Pillow Princess

Lock Down Publications and Ca$h Presents

Pillow Princess

A Novel by *S. Hawkins*

Lock Down Publications
Po Box 944
Stockbridge, Ga 30281

Visit our website @
www.lockdownpublications.com

Lock Down Publications
Like our page on Facebook: Lock Down Publications @
www.facebook.com/lockdownpublications.ldp
Book interior design by: **Shawn Walker**
Edited by: **Kiera Northington**

Stay Connected with Us!

Text **LOCKDOWN** to 22828 to stay up-to-date with new releases, sneak peaks, contests and more…
Thank you.

Submission Guideline.

Submit the first three chapters of your completed manuscript to ldpsubmissions@gmail.com, subject line: Your book's title. The manuscript must be in a .doc file and sent as an attachment. Document should be in Times New Roman, double spaced and in size 12 font. Also, provide your synopsis and full contact information. If sending multiple submissions, they must each be in a separate email.

Have a story but no way to send it electronically? You can still submit to LDP/Ca$h Presents. Send in the first three chapters, written or typed, of your completed manuscript to:

LDP: Submissions Dept
Po Box 944
Stockbridge, Ga 30281

DO NOT send original manuscript. Must be a duplicate.

Provide your synopsis and a cover letter containing your full contact information.

Thanks for considering LDP and Ca$h Presents.

S. Hawkins

Prologue
If It Isn't Love

Jessica peered at her beautiful reflection as she sat in front of the vanity mirror, swaying her hips to the Summer Walker lyrics in the background while applying her makeup. It was something she did every morning before she left the house. The smell of vanilla filled the room, setting the vibe. Parlay watched his fiancée from across the room.

"Good morning, love," he whispered as he leaned over and passionately kissed her forehead.

"Hey you," she said, turning completely around to face him. She extended her arms and wrapped them around his neck. His Versace Dylan Blue cologne brushed her nostrils, sending waves to her box. She pressed her thick lips against his, releasing a soft moan in the process. They stared at each other in complete admiration. Jessica was the best thing a man of his caliber could ask for. She had been there with him from the beginning.

"I'll be back tomorrow around this time," he said, buttoning up his white linen shirt, which displayed the exquisite artwork on his belly. His neatly-trimmed mustache highlighted his heart-shaped lips and his neatly-trimmed chin hair hung down to his Adam's apple. He had the type of smile that would take your breath away, pearly whites on the top row and a row of golds decorating the bottom.

"You promise?" Jessica asked without breaking her stare.

"I promise." He leaned down and kissed her lips again. He leaned up, removed a stack from the duffle bag, then zipped it up. "Go shopping. Enjoy yourself." He handed her the money.

Jessica beamed with joy. Slowly, she stood to her feet. A blind man could see the lust inside her big brown eyes.

Parlay's 6'2" frame hovered over her 5'3" frame. He leaned down and they shared a kiss as Jessica massaged his dick through his cargo shorts. She unzipped his shorts, reached inside his briefs, and pulled his dick out. Her mouth begin to salivate. Parlay was reddish-brown and his pole was a shade darker than his complexion. His thickness excited her. *If only I can get this motherfucka to come alive.* Jessica ran her tongue across her top lip before dropping to her knees. He unbuttoned his linen shirt again to get a clear view of what was about to happen. He watched as Jessica choked his dick with one hand, then slowly stroked it with the other. She wrapped her full lips around him, slowly swirling her tongue around his tip before removing both hands and swallowing him whole. Slowly, she made the dick vanish, then reappear, yet it still wasn't enough to stiffen his semi-erect dick.

Slurps and moans filled the room as Jessica cupped and messaged his balls to entice him even more. Parlay enjoyed every second of it as Jessica slowly bobbed her head up and down, licking the sides of the shaft before swallowing the whole thing. With the tip of his dick poking the back of the throat, she hummed loudly. The slight vibration with a tad bit of suction sent a wave of shock through his body that made his knees buckle slightly.

"Ooooh," he sounded as he began to slowly thrust forward.

She sucked and slurped slowly. She could feel Parlay tightening his ass cheeks. She knew what time it was. She bobbed back and forth even faster.

He moaned. "I'm cumming." The strain in his voice only revealed the intensity of what was brewing. He threw his head back in pleasure as he gripped the back of her head and thrust himself into her mouth. "Aaagh," he moaned as a nice size of glob shot into the back of her throat.

Jessica slurped it dry, then repeatedly tapped his tool against her tongue to rid it of anything that was left. She put his tool back inside his briefs and zipped his shorts.

Parlay helped her to her feet as he shook his head slowly. "Yo' ass gon' be the death of me." He smiled, wagging his finger in her face. He scooped her off her feet, cuffing her plump ass. "You so fucking sexy."

"You're so fucking handsome, and you're so good to me." She leaned in and kissed him.

After kissing, he placed her on her feet. Parlay stared into Jessica's natural honey-colored, almond-shaped eyes. Her complexion was the color of peanut butter. It was also smooth and free of blemishes. The forty-inch lace wig could've been a down payment for a brand new car. However, it gave Jessica an exotic touch. The fine, curly baby hairs lay perfectly along her forehead. She was simply gorgeous.

"You deserve the world and everything in it," he spoke, loosening his grip.

"Be safe. I'll be right here waiting on you," she said as she stood on her tiptoes to give him a peck on the lips.

Parlay smacked her ass and squeezed it, then headed out of the door. "I love you, Jess," Parlay said as he opened the door to exit.

"I love you too, Lay," she voiced, applying blush to her cheeks.

Seconds passed, and unbeknownst to Jessica, Parlay was still standing there. He just needed one last glance. Just one. Jessica slowly turned her head toward him, catching him staring. That sexy, boyish grin instantly made her smile. Parlay looked away, then quickly made his exit. Jessica sighed deeply, set her makeup brush down, then jumped to her feet. Quietly, she opened the door to make sure Parlay hadn't turned around.

The long hallway was empty as she swiveled her head in both directions. She closed the door, removing her robe as she raced to the California King-sized bed. Her clitoris pulsated in desperation. Jessica was filled with a gang of emotions. She was mad at Parlay for being selfish, steady taking the Xanax, knowing they were the reason his dick wouldn't harden. She was upset with herself for being such a materialistic bitch and settling for the money, knowing damn well she was in need of some sexual healing.

The thick, sticky liquid stretched from one leg to the other as she slowly parted her thick thighs. Oral sex with Parlay always opened her floodgates. She scrolled through her iPhone. There was a video in her phone that she kept. It was a video of her and Parlay going at it like honeymooners before his pill habit became an addiction. She hit the play button. The sight of Parlay's hard dick made her pussy throb even harder. She had never been sexed by anyone as good as Parlay before all the madness.

Parlay's entire family died in front of him, leaving him with a terrible case of anxiety. In the beginning, he would pop the pill occasionally. The state of bliss was nothing like he ever felt. But, after witnessing death himself, the pill became his crutch. Having knowledge of it all, Jessica remained by his side like the true rider she was without infidelity, lies, or questions. However, she did dwell often on how great it'd be if her sexual frustrations ceased.

Jessica twirled her fingers around the juices that coated her thigh. She licked the juices off her fingers, savoring the sweet taste. She reached in between her legs and easily coated them again and started rubbing her clit. She thought about every time Parlay hit her with "heart skip a beat" strokes.

"Ooohhh," she purred.

Jessica gently tapped her vagina, her clit growing with every tap. Jessica could feel heat brushing her toes. She began to pant. She then applied pressure to herself and slowly stroked herself in slow, circular motions. She sped up slightly. She bit down on her lip so hard she was sure she had drawn blood as her body begin to jerk violently. She exploded, feeling the warm liquid stream down the crack of her ass.

S. Hawkins

Chapter 1
Meet Me at the Altar

Cars lined the parking lot of the church, a few luxury and a few normal. It was a gathering of made niggas, paid bitches, and simply well-respected figures throughout the community.

Parlay stared at himself in the full-length mirror as he straightened his bow tie. His head glistened as he palmed the waves on his fresh bald fade. His mustache and chin hair were shaped and lined up to perfection as well. His perfectly-tailored Armani suit was all white, fitting him impeccably. is expensive chain decorated his neck, slightly swinging from side to side as it draped directly in the center of his chest.

Today was the big day. He was marrying the woman that made his soul smile. Parlay was in the presence of his team, and even though they talked amongst each other, it felt like he was the only man in the room. Parlay was the plug - well, he was the plug in Texas. He flooded the streets of Dallas, Houston, Austin and any of the outskirt cities nearby. However, Parlay was very low-key and calculated. He moved slowly and with precision.

Nothing happens fast but a crash.

His pops would always say, and for that reason alone, he moved slow. He was calm and lax. No one ever witnessed him raise his voice, nor did he move to any tune but his own. He made demands. You either followed them or fell off.

The door opened and everyone paused and turned their heads in that direction. Parlay calmly peered through the mirror. He faintly smirked at his right-hand man as Prime strolled in his direction.

"Today's the day! My nigga is a married man now," Prime said proudly with his arm thrown around Parlay's shoulder. Prime was dark-skinned with a slim build. He stood about six foot even and he rocked a low, tapered fade. He was from Brooklyn, New York, and it was obvious in his style. He had moved to Texas seven years ago to follow his mother. He had found out that she suffered from breast cancer and needed a caretaker. She promised him that she'd be fine after the chemotherapy.

Prime held on to that, like he had always done with his mother's words. Oblivious to the severity of her health, he made plans to return to Brooklyn once she was done with chemo. However, Prime's mother died shortly thereafter and he never made it back to the place where he was birthed. He stayed and pursued the drug game. He met Parlay and they had been tight ever since He was the C.O.O. and Parlay was the C.E.O. Parlay never got his hands dirty, and Prime never liked his hands clean.

Prime leaned in closer. "Fam, on the real, I need to rap with you about something." He locked eyes with his protégé, conveying his concern.

Parlay cleared his throat. "Give me and Prime a few minutes alone." He didn't yell, yet everybody in the room heard him loud and clear.

The room cleared out instantly as Parlay waited for the last one to close the door. Once the door was shut, he peered back at Prime. Both of the men slyly slid their hands in their slacks simultaneously.

"You know they found Quinton dead at his baby mother's house early this morning," Prime said, then lowered his head.

Parlay frowned in utter disbelief. "What Quinton?" he questioned.

"Quinton that runs the spot in the cliff."

Parlay gritted his teeth in anger. His eyes narrowed further as he mouth disappeared into a tight straight line. He clenched his fist in frustration. He wanted to roar, or perhaps even break

14

something, yet he kept his cool. Losing control meant weakening his discipline, and there was no way he could lose something he had to worked so hard to attain. The loss of Quinton struck him deeply. Quinton was the son of his close friend Reem. Reem was currently doing time in a federal prison out West. Even though they didn't share the same bloodline, they were family by the way of the drug game.

"He wasn't shot or anything." Prime paused. "Fucking with them fake P's. They were laced with fentanyl," Prime added while shaking his head.

Parlay knew that Prime hated the fact that he was addicted to the Xanax. However, the truth of the matter is, he simply couldn't stop if he wanted to. It had been a week since he looked at a Xanax. Jessica had been patient and selfless with him, so he wanted to reward her with some good, long, love-making in return.

"Don't worry, young'un. I'm easing my way off of this shit. Watch in a few months." Parlay patted his back.

Just as Prime was about to respond, the door swung open and Jessica's mother came in. She rocked a gray pixie cut, which perfectly shaped her round face. Her face was made up and she was clad in an evening gown that matched the color of the wedding.

"Hey Momma," Parlay said. The very words triggered his anxiety, yet he clenched his teeth in an attempt to keep it together.

She smiled from ear to ear. "Come on. Pastor is ready for you."

Parlay respectfully made his way towards her and the three of them headed towards the exit and to the main chapel. Parlay was filled with mixed emotions as he headed to the chapel. He was elated to make Jessica his wife. However, Quinton's death lay heavily on his heart. Quinton was the fourth person he knew this month that died from the fentanyl-laced pills. Fear surfaced, then vanished as quickly as he blinked his eyes. Parlay had no worries since his Xanax were prescribed, straight from the doctor's office. There was no way he was going to deal with someone on the streets and gamble with his life. He took a deep breath. Slowly, he walked up the stairs and through the massive French-style opening.

Jessica walked through the doors. She walked down the long hallway with her girls in tow. It was time. She was clad in a flowing dress that hugged every curve her mother blessed her with. It was the most beautiful and exquisite dress the guests had ever laid eyes on. The sheer, tube-like dress was tight fitting all the way down. The train on her dress dragged a few feet behind her. Her makeup artist followed her and held up the rear of her dress. Jessica's face was beat to the gods. The violet lipstick was the icing on the cake. She was absolutely beautiful.

The line of groomsmen and bridesmaids stood at the crown of the church. Prime and Parlay smiled and whispered to each other while waiting for the bride to enter. The music kicked in and everyone stood to their feet. Everyone's eyes shot to the entrance as they waited anxiously for the bride to appear. Jamie Foxx's "Fall for your Type" lyrics pumped out of the speakers.

The music tugged at her heartstrings as she closed her eyes. *Stay calm, you good. Do not mess up your makeup!* Since she had picked every décor, she chose every setup and she had even picked the suit Parlay wore. She gave him the option of choosing the song that broached her presence and sealed their love forever.

He remembered.

Tears burned the back of Jessica's eyes as she blinked rapidly to snap out of the awed state she was in. Four years ago, before the two of them even had a label, Jessica had mentioned to Parlay just how much she loved the song, how it touched her soul and tugged at her heart strings. Moreso, she clearly remembered telling him that whenever she would marry, that would be the song she'd choose. The way he made her feel, words couldn't describe. He may have been addicted to Xans, yet her addiction was him.

Suddenly, the large church doors swung open. Jessica stood there as everyone peered back at her in amazement. Gasps and chatter filled the room. Jessica made her way down the aisle, her beautiful smile and gorgeous face exposed as she slowly strutted towards her man. They hadn't even spoken their vows yet, but neither of them could wait for the honeymoon.

S. Hawkins

Chapter 2
They Diking

"I wanna drive you crazy
Pull up inside me, baby, fuck a nigga up like oopsy daisy, ain't
no if, and, buts, and maybe
Don't be laid up in that shit like you lazy
I need you to roll up in that shit like you lazy
I need you to roll up in that shit like you skating
Baby, ain't no hold up. I'm the shit. I hate waiting..."

Normani pumped out of the speakers as Jah held a large bottle of champagne in her hand and gazed at the beauty on stage. Reclined comfortably in the seat with her legs outstretched, she seldomly peered down at her iWatch, awaiting her time to clock out. Jah was short for Jah'lia. She was a certified barber during the day and at night, she pushed P's and whatever else she could get her hands on. Certified was more of a term and not simply used because she was licensed. Jah was truly certified with her skills. Her clientele list with her "cutz" alone was longer than the Sweet Georgia Brown line Sundays. Walk-ins were accepted as long as you were cool with the wait.

"I'm closing shop in ten minutes, and then I'm on my way home," she spoke into the receiver to the only woman that had her heart. "Okay, bae, I can't wait." Whenever they were apart, the two of them acted as if they hadn't seen each other in days. A smile etched Jah's face as she ended the call. Her smile began to fade as the beauty on stage slowly made her way down the steps into her direction. As she got closer, her pace slowed, adding a deeper sway in her hips. "You so cute," she bragged, finger-combing her hair with her four-inch nails.

Her full lips and made-up face made her resemble a black Barbie Doll. Her smooth dark skin glistened. Her two-piece left little to the imagination, turning Jah on instantly.

"'Preciate ya."

Jah had been a stud since middle school. Her voice had naturally and gradually equipped a hint of masculinity. She licked her full pink lips, then rough massaged her hand on top and around her sponge-fro. Her line up was sharp and the fade was crisp and blended immaculately. Her legs were crossed at the ankles as she stood before Jah like a schoolgirl with a crush.

"I'm about to head out in about five minutes." Jah yawned, then stood to her feet, stretching her arms. She stood at 5'7". Tattoos covered her entire body, yet her Amiri jogging suit concealed all of them besides the roman numerals on her neck. The tattoo was fire red with black shading around it, embellishing her sexy but rugged look. Her honey golden skin glowed under the eccentric lighting.

"I bet you taste good," she said, tracing her lips with her tongue. She took Jah's smile as an acceptance to her invitation. Without uttering another word, she headed to the room that they referred to as the greenlight special. Jah trailed slowly.

Jah panted quick, short breaths as the stripper chick attacked her love button with expertise. Jah sat on the cushioned bench reclined against the wall, one leg east and the other one west. With one hand, Jah used her middle and index finger to pull back the fat that slightly hovered over her throbbing magic spot. The stripper placed her hands on her knees while slowly massaging Jah's clit in circular motions. The sight of Jah's wet, fat pussy made her clitoris throb in desperation, leaving her no choice but to touch it. She slurped her blooming bud, then peered up at Jah.

Jah was a sucka for some good top. She slurped a few more times, then flickered her tongue across her button at a rapid speed. Her fingers moved even quicker. Her breaths quickened. The warm air brushing her clit made Jah bite down on her lip. She wanted to reach back and punch her ass, the shit felt so good.

"Ugh," Jah moaned. Her stomach and ass cheeks tightened as a powerful orgasm threatened to emerge. Veins protruded from her neck as sweat decorated Jah's forehead.

"Aagh," the stripper moaned sexily. Her tongue ceased for that moment. Her body slightly jerked as she worked her hand oddly fast.

Jah's head swiveled left to right as she tried enduring without exploding. However, it was no use. The chick's tongue moved with precision. She worked her spot like she made it. She didn't budge; not even a little. Jah squeezed her legs tight, blocking her airwaves, and shorty still didn't stop.

"Aaargghh!" Jah loosened her grip completely while panting breathlessly, pushing her head away from her sensitivity. "Gotdamn," Jah whispered.

It had been almost a month since she had gotten some head. She was so keen on overly satisfying her woman that there was never enough energy for another bust. Either way, Jah was satisfied. She would bust just from penetrating her lady. But, every now and then, she could use some good ol' sloppy top. It wasn't anything in comparison.

"My turn" the stripper voiced, removing the clamp that held the bikini top together.

"Hell yeah! I want to taste your sexy ass," Jah said while rubbing her hands together.

"Let me take a piss real quick."

She jumped to her feet. The burst of energy was sudden. "Have that pussy ready for me."

Jah climbed into the seat of her 2018 Camaro. She whipped her phone out and called her lady while bringing the engine alive. She sped out of the lot and into traffic. "Hey lady." Jah's tone was low, almost whisper-like. She was barely three minutes past due, and she needed to put her mind at ease before it began to wander. Monique's temper was like a bubble. It took a little of nothing for it to burst.

"Hey you, you on your way?"

"Didn't I tell you I was?" Jah paused. "Isn't it past ten minutes?" she continued sarcastically.

Monique smashed her lips. "You right," she admitted. Monique placed her feet in the air as she lay comfortably on her stomach. The TV was the only light that illuminated the living room besides the lit candle that sat atop the fireplace and filled the room with a subtle but lingering lavender scent.

"Alright then," Jah voiced before ending the call.

Within ten minutes, she was pulling into the driveway of the three-bedroom home that she and Monique shared. She threw the car in park, then reached underneath the passenger seat. She pulled out the container of off-brand baby wipes and yanked two out. Monique was sharp as a tick. There wasn't nothing she could get past her, so she wasn't going to even try. With one hand, she lifted her briefs and jogging pants, giving her a clear view of her pussy. She covered two of her fingers with the wipes and thoroughly cleaned and dried her wet pussy. She eyed the wet sticky shit on the wipe and grinned. *Man, shawty had some fiya.* She stepped out of her car and walked to the end of the driveway. She lifted the lid of the trash bin and tossed the wet wipes inside. Jah was a head hunter. She would lay the wood depending on the female, opportunity, and mood she was in. However, she made sure nothing ever got back to Monique and she never stuck around long enough to catch feelings. Like a trained fighter, she would stick and move.

Her eyes shifted in every direction as she tried locating Monique inside of the dark bedroom.

"Hey you," Monique greeted. She switched on the dim light across the room exposing what was once hidden.

Jah's jaw dropped at the sight of the stallion moving towards her. Clad in neon green lingerie, she looked simply stunning with the exotic one-piece accentuating her curves. Her large D-cup breasts, slim waist, and thick thighs made her chocolate goodies look edible, and Jah's mouth begin to salivate.

"I got something for you," she spoke in the sexiest voice and then wrapped her arms around Jah's neck.

Monique stood at 5'5". Jah had her by merely a few inches. Jah grinned, exposing that beautiful smile that Monique loved so much. She squeezed both of her plump cheeks that hung from underneath the sheer dress.

"Oooohh," Jah moaned.

Everything about Monique screamed sensual. Her cat like hazel eyes and the way a few of her dreads hung down her back and on the side of her face from her well put together, messy bun got Jah every time.

Monique led Jah to the thick multicolored blanket that nearly covered the entire living room. Bottles of bubbly, fruit, and two plates of seafood sat amongst it. Jah immediately stripped down to nothing but her sports bra and Ethika briefs. Her belly slightly protruded past the waist band. However, her V-cut was still quite noticeable.

It's the V-cut for me, Monique, thought staring at Jah with a slight grin. Monique loved Jah. She was her centerpiece. Her imperfections didn't need any corrections. She loved her in her rarest form. Monique may have assumed that her outer beauty was what got Jah, but was the inner beauty for her.

She was the most intelligent woman Jah had met. She was from the city, but there were many things that separated her from the rest of the chicks around the way. She wasn't bougie and didn't see herself better than the next. She simply separated herself from anything detrimental to her growth, morals, and values. With the level of ambition she possessed, you would've thought she was raised under the most poverty-stricken conditions, but she wasn't. They weren't that great, but they weren't so bad either.

Jah stared at Monique in admiration.

"What, bae? Sit down."

Jah sat down Indian style directly across from Monique. "I love you," Jah said confidently, half smiling as she reached over and swept the dreads behind her ear.

"I love you more," she replied as a huge smile spread across her face, displaying her perfect white teeth. The violet purple lipstick stunningly highlighted them.

The room went silent besides the soft John Legend song that played at a low volume. They may have not been moving their mouths, yet their eyes told it all. They were looking at their other half, the person that made them each whole. Jah leaned in for a deep but passionate kiss. She ended it with a soft peck on the lips. She stood up and grabbed a bottle of champagne out of the bucket of ice that sat on the ledge. She picked it up and popped the cork, causing a small volcano-like eruption. She filled Monique's glass halfway and then guzzled the expensive liquid straight from the bottle.

Monique stood to her feet. She removed her robe, exposing nothing but that sheer dress. She walked up to Jah and grabbed the bottle out of her hand, taking her own swig. Monique placed the bottle on the ledge and laid on top of the blanket. She opened her thick thighs. Jah licked her lips once her fat vagina lips came into view. The studded diamond that decorated the top of her pussy made it even more edible. Jah took another swig, unsure if she wanted to dive in and feast or go and get Mister.

Mister was the name Monique had given her strap a few years ago when they first start dating. It was a shade darker than Jah. Nine inches long, the thickness was overwhelming, and there was even a thick vein that ran from the base to the beginning of the tip.

"Go get 'em," Monique whined seductively as she moaned softly, rubbing her breasts through her dress. They were big, round and supple. She didn't have on a bra, so her hard nipples were certainly noticeable through the neon dress.

Jah returned wearing nothing but the strap. Monique's tight tunnel was extremely wet. Jah slowly fell to her knees, opening her legs further apart so she could slide in. Monique's juicy vagina lips were glazed and her erect clitoris was pulsating. She snatched the dress over her head so that her full body was on display. Jah grabbed both of her legs and gently pushed them back to the point where both of her feet were over her head. Jah slowly slid inside of her and begin to grind in hard, slow, circular motions. She moaned in pleasure as Jah grinded inside of her.

"Oooohh, please don't stop," she begged for more, gazing up at Jah lustfully as she rotated her hips, matching her thrusts.

Monique was an all-out freak. Jah loved that side to her. The sound of her wetness was as if someone was stirring creamy pasta. Their rhythm was in complete unison. Jah plunged into her love over and over, doing her damndest to hit her with her best strokes. After a minute of nonstop thrusting, they both felt a release brewing, whispering how good it felt to one another. They stared into each other's eyes, conveying every emotion they felt for one another.

Jah leaned back, slid her hands underneath her plump ass cheeks, and spread them apart. She jabbed her box harder and faster as she felt an explosion coming.

"Don't stop, bae, I'm cumming!"

She closed her eyes and her love came. Her legs began to shake and her toes curled as she let it all go. Monique felt a gush of fluid shoot from her and for a few seconds, she was dazed. Oddly, she had lost all control over her body movements and she quivered like she had never done before.

Once she was done cumming, Jah slid out of her. She removed the strap, tossing it aside. She used two fingers and slid them around her dripping wet opening, instantly drenching her fingers. She leaned in and Monique opened her mouth, ready to awaken her taste buds. She found it absurd that Jah's pussy got wetter than hers, and she was the one getting fucked. She smacked as she savored the flavor of Jah's juices. It was as if Jah's juices gave her energy. Her once-drained body was filled and she felt capable again. She eased onto her knees.

"Let me eat that dick."

Chapter 3
So Deep in My Feelings

Jessica and Diamond sat at one of the tables inside of the shopping mall enjoying a Chick-Fil-A meal. She hadn't had the opportunity to spend the money Parlay had given her, so she figured today would be the perfect day to do so since he was expected to return tonight. Chatter and laughter echoed throughout the mall, but the volume wasn't overwhelming. Diamond effortlessly detected her friend's vibe in spite of the constant smile and laughter. Diamond used the napkin to remove the grease that glazed her freshly manicured nails.

"Talk to me, bitch," Diamond said while sucking her teeth.

Jessica gave her a blank stare. She didn't think the feelings and mental anguish she tried so hard to conceal were so obvious. But then again, no one knew her like Diamond knew her.

Diamond and Jessica had been friends since elementary. The only time they separated as adolescents was the few times Diamond went to Juvenile for running away from home. The abuse that her stepfather would inflict upon her mother was too much for her eyes. Finally, her mother agreed to letting her finish the school year at Jessica's. Diamond didn't just stay at Jessica's that year, but up until they were seniors in high school. Their senior year, the girls moved out and into a two-bedroom townhome of their own. A year after Jessica met Parlay was the moment the women separated. Their addresses may have changed, but everything else remained the same, like their imperishable bond.

"Your pussy-bumping ass wouldn't understand." Jessica grinned, then crossed her arms over her chest.

Diamond didn't know if it was the things she watched her stepfather do to her mother that made her despise men or if perhaps she truly had an attraction for women. Either way, she got herself involved in a relationship with the same sex since she was able to shave her pussy. There was something unique about a woman that Diamond found so enticing.

"This isn't about me. It's about you," Diamond said, staring at Jessica sternly.

She lowered her head. "It's Parlay," she admitted. She sighed deeply as if it pained her to touch on such subject, but the topic isn't what pained her. Her suffering was what frustrated her to a point she could possibly never attain again.

As soon as Parlay's name fell from Jessica's lips, Diamond lowered her head. She was cognizant of the significant amount of love she had for him, and she feared the depths that her friend would go.

"Remember…" Jessica paused, scooting her chair close. "Remember I told you about the situation with our sex life, right?

Diamond nodded her head quickly, immediately replaying the past conversation in her head.

Jessica sighed deeply. "I'm sexually frustrated, D. But I love him." She placed her hand over her heart as tears welled in her eyes.

"Oooh, baby, I can't even imagine how you must feel, 'cause I get this kitty stroked every night," she joked, patting the top of her pussy.

Jessica burst out in laughter, lightening her dampened spirit. "Ugh! Your gay ass is so nasty," Jessica said using her finger to dab her eyes.

"Don't knock it until you try it."

Jessica peered at her through eyes of disgust. Her scowl resembled someone who had just eaten something distasteful.

"Look." Diamond paused. She placed her elbows on the table, using her forearms to elevate her perky breasts as she leaned in. Her thin lips resembled a folded sheet of paper, however, they looked softer than clouds. The small sapphire Diamond had in the middle of her bottom lip highlighted them, almost making you look past their odd size. "We gonna check your pussy meter," Diamond said.

Jessica scowled. "What the hell is that?" she inquired. Knowing Diamond, she probably had some freaky gay shit in mind. Just mentioning it would be the reason Jessica terminated the entire discussion.

"Let's go out——"

"I'm not going to any of those gay-ass clubs with you. I don't want to see no studs slow dancing or any trans twerking and pole dancing," she said with bite, crossing her arms over her chest.

"Damn, bitch, I know you don't like pussy! With your strictly dickly ass." She held up her hand and curled her middle and index underneath.

The bisexual shit was never Jessica's hype, and on every set, she let it be known. Her hatred was stronger than any addiction, and no matter how hard she tried, she simply couldn't shake the feeling. "Okay, so what's the play?"

"We going out, and you'll know if it's really sexual frustration the way your pussy responds when you're around attractive men." She shrugged. "Maybe you just need to get out the house a little."

S. Hawkins

Chapter 4
Somebody That I Used to Know

Prime was leaned up against the car conversing with a beautiful mixed woman. He noticed Parlay coming his way and cut the conversation short.

"It's all there," Parlay smoothly said as he slid a toothpick in his mouth.

"Get paid, young nigga, get paid," Prime responded as he slapped hands with his close friend.

Parlay walked around to the passenger side of the car and hopped inside. The duffle he had come with was left behind in the shabby basement of the five-star establishment, yet the order he just placed was signed, sealed, and waiting for him at a secluded location inside of his city.

"Look, I know you a businessman and you ready to get back so that you can handle your business, but bruh, I just need about twenty minutes top with that baddie I was just talking to," he said, then nodded towards the thick mixed breed that stood a few feet away from the car, pretending to be deeply involved with whoever she was peering down at on her phone.

"It ain't no pressure. Handle your business. Matter of fact…" Parlay paused, retrieving his phone from his pocket, remember the food joint in the ATL everyone had been talking about. He never once tried vegan meals, but everyone was talking about the new joint and he just had to see what the hype was about.

Prime rubbed his hands together in excitement.

"You a trip, bruh. I can't stick my dick in nothing without having a mental connection," Parlay said while searching for the address to the restaurant.

"I figured you would say that. That's why I didn't mention her sister," Prime responded, then let out a chuckle.

Parlay grinned while shaking his head. He knew he had seen the ad for the restaurant on Facebook but for some reason, he couldn't find it. "Yeah, I'm good on all that, li'l bro, but aye, run me up here and I'm going to chill and eat while you do your thing."

"Bet."

"Li'l baby!" Prime continued waving the girl over.

She pushed her phone down into her denim shorts. They were so short they stopped just below her coochie lips. The denim material was so tight and thin you could see the print of her fat pussy lips.

Prime licked his lips as he watched the pretty young thing strut in his direction. Her legs were long, thick, and blemish free. The sun had tanned her banana-colored skin, making it look a golden honey color. She was about 5'6" with a waist that could've belonged to a ten-year-old. Her pretty, brown round nipples were visible through her thin peach-colored baby doll tee, exposing the diamond that glistened and hung from her belly button. Her tight eyes and high cheekbones made her look foreign. She wore her tight curls pulled tightly into a high bun giving her face the lift women paid top dollar for. A few of the curls hung loosely at the back. She licked her heart-shaped lips as she walked up on Prime, invading his personal space.

"So I'm leaving with you or what?" she asked with her hands rested on her hips. She popped her bubble gum, exposing the two flat diamonds that decorated the top of her tongue.

Seeing the tongue piercing immediately aroused him. He flicked the top of his nose, then grabbed his dick, lifting the middle of his Jordan basketball shorts. "Hell yeah! Tell your sister she can go do her thing I'll take you home." Prime licked his lips as he undressed the cutie with his eyes.

She turned around and chucked her sister the deuces. He assumed that was her signal to leave because shorty drove off shortly after.

"Get in. That's my bro, but I'm about to drop him off," Prime said, opening the door for her.

"How you doing?" Parlay asked, but it sounded more like a statement. He never even peered up from his phone to peep shortly. Unbeknownst, to her Parlay had already gotten an eyeful. True enough, shorty was a baddie, but she wasn't his baddie and he didn't want anything that wasn't his - pussy include.

"Heeyy," she responded with a hint of extra friendliness in her voice.

Prime turned the volume up and proceeded to his destination.

"I'm not talking the weekend, but I'm talking 'bout Abel
You see the shit that Cain did and they wasn't even strangers
(damn)
My daddy dead, my mama dead
So God, send me some angels…"

The Gucci Mane lyrics begin to fade as Prime slowed in front of the restaurant. Parlay opened the door. His phone vibrated, ceasing his movement. He peered down at the screen. He wanted to burst out in laughter, but squinted instead. He pretended to be reading the text. He was really focusing on keeping a straight face. Unbeknownst to shorty in the back ,it was a text from Prime.

Don't forget.

A reminder so that he would remember to say the rehearsal line before making his exit. On several occasions similar to the one today, Prime would manage to meet a chick with plans to have his way with her. Some he would have to promise a little more to get what he wanted. Shorty must have been one of those, Parlay assumed as soon as he received the text. The famous line was meant to penetrate the woman's mental so that she would already know her time with Prime was limited so that she'd keep the bullshit and conversation to a minimum.

"Aye, that was bae. You know how she is. Don't have me waiting on you forever. Make sure you back in thirty minutes," Parlay announced seriously, placing one foot on the cement.

Prime sucked his teeth, pretending to be bothered. "Alright, fam, you know I got you. Climb up front, shorty."

Parlay closed the door behind him. He stepped on top of the curb and gazed at the establishment before walking inside. The setting inside was very homely with a feminine touch. It was a mixture of a southern cafe and a soul food joint. Parlay liked the vibe and he hadn't even sat down yet. He sighed deeply, seeing the hostess walking his direction.

"Hi, welcome to Lettie's Veggies. Is there anywhere specific you'd like to be seated?"

Parlay peered around at the semi-packed room. He spotted a spot in the rear of the establishment that was beside one of the many huge windows facing the busy streets of Atlanta. "I'll take that one over there." Parlay pointed

"Woooh." She paused. The hostess had caught a whiff of his Versace cologne. It was strong, but subtle, and it matched his fly. Parlay was clad in multicolored Palm Angels V-neck and black shorts that fell about five inches above his knees, the ones most golfers wore. He was comfortably dressed and seemingly plain to those who weren't hipped to the latest fashion. She placed a hand over her chest, stunned by the alluring smell that stirred her insides suddenly.

Parlay grinned. "What's wrong?"

Her light skin turned beet red as she locked eyes with him. "Nothing. You just smell so good, that's all." She sighed deeply.

Parlay's smile never faded as he shook his head while following behind her to his seat. She handed him the menu and promise to return shorty. Parlay stared down at the reasonable menu. The food samples looked magically delicious, but even Parlay knew looks could be deceiving. Seeing the name of the restaurant scribbled across the menu, his heart smiled matching the half smile plastered on his handsome face.

He met a lady name Letty once. She was an older woman. Her heart was pure as gold. She was the most hospitable person he ever met in the thirty-one years he lived on earth. He was a close friend of her granddaughter's, which was the way he was formally introduced to the elderly woman in the first place. He hadn't seen Ms. Letty or her granddaughter since the summer of his freshman year in high school. However, it still didn't change a thing. Even if he saw the woman ten years from now, he would never forget her nor her amazing characteristics.

Parlay was unsure about what he should order. It all looked amazing. A different chick approached his table.

"Hi, I'll be your server today. My name is Kayla. How may I help you?" Kayla's ebony skin was darker than most, but smoother than butter. She had very inviting eyes and a big warm and friendly smile.

"Um." Parlay paused, making his mouth disappear then reappear. He chuckled softly. "I really don't know what to order it's my first time visiting. I couldn't help but to check it out. I constantly hear nothing but good things about the place."

She gasped dramatically. It was a little over the top. "You're going to love it here! From the staff to the food, the vibes…" She leaned down. "You should try the burger with fries," she suggested.

Parlay's brows dipped in confusion as he dwelled on the mystery of it all. *How the hell is it vegan?* Although he was a bit hesitant, he agreed anyways.

"Can I get a glass of ice water?" Parlay peered around in every direction, admiring the scenery.

"Um." She narrowed her eyes as she tried to figure out the answer to his question. She looked around for help, anyone who could possibly assist the handsome man seated in front of her.

"Hey there's my boss right there. How about we ask her?" she voiced, beaming with joy as she pointed to the woman behind her, who stood out amongst the crowed. It was as if a light shone directly above her head in an area surrounded by darkness. "Boss lady!" Her head swirled from left to right. Kayla waved her hand, grabbing her attention.

Everything about the chick was smooth, from the way she tossed her hair over her shoulders to the sway of her hips. Parlay flashed his famous smile and then it slightly faded.

Her brows furrowed. "Parlay?" she asked.

"Natasha?" he inquired, leaping down his feet.

Simultaneously, they wrapped their arms around each other., each of their scents brushing against one another's nostrils, and they both found the similar fragrances quite pleasurable.

"Wow, look at you." She stood back. Both her hands rested on her hips as she took her time taking inventory, an asset at a time.

"You look good yourself," Parlay shot back. His mental immediately recapped the days he worshipped the ground Natasha walked on. She was the most popular female freshman. Her body was hypnotizing; her moves was sick. She was lit. There was no better way to describe her.

"Nah, you got me beat," she said.

Natasha was extremely attractive. She was stacked with perky breasts, a slim waist, firm ass, and smooth dark chocolate skin. Her bundles were long and wavy. The copper highlights complimented the rich brown, which highlighted her honey-colored, almond-shaped eyes. However, it was the lips for Parlay. She had the sexiest lips ever. They were full, but not too big, with the dip in the middle of her top lip. The thin coat of gloss made them look even more appealing. Parlay looked away to silence his thoughts.

"How's Ms. Letty?" Just the thought of her brought a smile to his face.

However, Natasha's tight-lipped smile spoke volumes.

Sensing her discomfort. Parlay pointed her to one of the chairs at his table.

"Where do I start?"

***

Meanwhile, on the other side of town, moans and grunts filled the spacious 2020 Cadillac Escalade. Prime had every intent to purchase a room in spite of the fact that he only had thirty minutes with the beauty. A nice suite for a day would display his appreciation. However, once she freed his pole from the mastery that kept it concealed and welcomed him into her warm, wet mouth the thought of getting a room vanished that very instant. It didn't stop him from climbing into the backseat.

"Shit," he spoke through clenched teeth as he squeezed his ass cheeks tight, hoping the rising of his bust would submerge. He curled his toes so tight cramps begin to shoot up his leg, but he wouldn't dare ask her to stop.

Pop!

Like the sound of a baby spitting his pacifier out, that's the sound that the chick's mouth and his penis made.

"Uh-uh. I want to see what that dick do," she said, seductively easing from the squatted position she had been in for the last ten minutes.

"That makes two of us. Let a nigga bust that li'l pussy open," he voiced smoothly, slowly moving his hand up and down his pole.

She bent down a bit to prevent her head from touching the roof of the truck. She shimmied out of the tight shorts, pulling the sheer thong down with them. Seeing her plump and pretty pussy made Prime's pole a bit harder. His dick was so hard it hurt as it wagged side to side like a dog's tail on its own. If it could talk, it would've sounded like Keith Sweat, and if it had all five of the senses, it would've cried. There wasn't an imperfection anywhere on her body. Effortlessly, she freed her perky breasts from the peach-colored top that only did so much to conceal them. Although Prime was facing her head on, the protrusion of her ass could be seen. Shorty was a slim, thick, stallion.

"Sit yo' ass on this monsta," Prime demanded, referring to his nine-inch pole.

The slight curve made her eyes gleam with excitement. She had never bounced on a crooked pole before. Slowly, she mounted him. Drops of her juices landed on his thigh as she positioned herself on top of him. She eased down. His tip knocked at her opening and before she could answer, he burst through her fleshly doors. She gasped sharply, his thickness stretching her pussy instantly. She bit down on her lip as she worked her way down his entire pole.

"This shit hurt so good," she said, her eyes closed as she enjoyed every second of the pleasurable feeling.

Prime shuddered once he was completely inside. Her pussy felt like a super tight mouth. It was warm, wet, and her walls were soft and plush like the thin sensitive flesh that was all around the inside of a human being's mouth. Not to mention, she was bad as fuck. A minute man wasn't even in his stats, but he was going to be one if she kept tugging and hugging his dick the way she did.

"Aye, hold on." He placed a death grip on her thighs to cease her movement. He moaned, lowering his head as she hit Kegels on his shit. A feeling so rewarding and profound fluttered in the center of his chest. *Damn*, he thought, because he struggled to say a word.

She giggled highly aware of what she was doing.

"Get up and ride it from the back," Prime managed to utter.

"I don't have to get up," she voiced before placing each leg behind her head and using his midsection to spin herself around. Once her back was to his, she didn't even give Prime enough time to make another request before she arched her back and rode his pole. She moved like a pro, and Prime matched her tune. This time he, couldn't stop what was threatening to emerge.

"I'm cummin'!" Even her whiny voice felt like music to Prime ears.

He was on the brink too. She sped up her pace, her ass making loud smacking noises every time she pounced down.

"Ugh!" Prime lifted shorty by her ass cheeks, enough to pull his pole out of her cave. He placed a tight hold on his dick, aiming it at the center of her back. His continuous grunts sounded like a bad motor inside of a vehicle. He placed a death drip around her neck, pulling her a little closer. The tip of his penis poked her in the back as the thick glob of liquid spewed out. Like the oil and the vibrator the therapist used at the massage parlor, he pressed his dick into his own goo as he swirled and stirred the mess.

"Shit." He exhaled. His breaths were quick and short as he tried to regain control of it.

She turned to face him, eyeing him from below as she rested on her knees. He swatted his dick against the palm of his hand. Thick drops of creamy shit fell into it.

"Give me that," she said in a childlike voice, her eyes overly inviting.

He stuck his hand out to where it was level with her mouth. Like a dog, she used her thick tongue to lick it clean. Prime gave her the most satisfying smile one could muster. He could tell just by peering into her irises that shorty was a track star, the type to restrain from falling for because her past had forced her to loosen any feelings connected to her heart strings. However, the temporary bliss outweighed the risk and he had every intent on taking it.

***

Parlay didn't even realize that Prime was ten minutes past his curfew, nor did he see him walk inside of the restaurant until he stood directly in front of his table.

"Aww shit." Parlay peered down at his watch. "My bad, li'l homie. This is Natasha, an old friend of mine." Parlay paused, allowing the two of them to formally greet.

"We been chopping it up 'bout the good ol' days and time flew by. My bad," he apologized.

"It's cool. I'm going to grab a table and get my grub on and we can leave then."

"Cool, cool, we can do that."

Prime walked off.

"Hey," Parlay called out, forcing him to stop and turn on his heels.

"Get the burger and fire. That shit was so damn good," he voiced, rubbing his stomach in a circular motion.

"Boy, your ass still the same. My grandmother would've loved to see you all grown up."

Parlay's smile faded. Inwardly, he wished the same thing. Ms. Letty was one of those people that you would do anything just to see that genuine smile of hers, to receive her warming acceptance. A "well done" would've been worth more than a million dollars coming from someone of her caliber.

"I know. I would've love to see her too. I wish we would've never lost contact. The least I could've done was attend her funeral and put the best flowers on her tombstone."

"You can still put those flowers on her tombstone."

Parlay lifted his head. His eyes gleamed with hope. "You right. I sure can do that."

"Well, I know you're about to head back to the D, but whenever you make the trip again, we'll go and see her together."

They both smiled, and locked eyes longer than they intended.

"Will do."

S. Hawkins

Chapter 5
Independent Bitches

"Hey gorgeous," Parlay complimented as he stood in the entry of the doorway to the bedroom he and Jessica shared.

"Aaagghh," she yelled loudly, leaping from the stool she was sitting on.

"I didn't even hear you come in. I missed you, zaddy!" she laid her head on his chest as she wrapped her arms around his mid-section tightly.

Parlay chuckled. "I missed you too, momma." He leaned down and wrapped his arms around her waist. He gripped her soft, plump ass and lifted her off her feet.

Jessica yelped in excitement. She loved it whenever he would do that. She leaned in and kissed his lips. They shared a slow and passionate kiss. It was evident that they both had missed one another.

Parlay placed her gently on her feet. "Where you going?" he asked. Jessica's face glowed from the highlights perfectly applied, so he knew she was stepping out. On a regular day, she would just go with a natural beat, but upon seeing the coral eyeshadow, he knew was something out the ordinary. Her coral eyeshadow matched the gloss she wore. She looked finger lickin' good. She wore a huge terry cloth robe with a towel wrapped around her head.

"Me and Diamond are hooking up. It's been a minute. We just having a little girls' night out," she said, not wanting to admit to much. Parlay was the only man Jessica had eyes for, and the last thing she wanted was to heighten his suspicion.

"Okay, okay, cool. I was just checking on you. But in a few minutes, me and Prime going to head out and handle some business," he said, referring to the shipment that was waiting for him at the designated location.

"Okay, bae, I'll see you when you get in. Make sure you and Prime eat before y'all leave," Jessica answered as she applied mascara to her lashes.

"Hell yeah. We grabbed a bite to eat before hitting the road, but I'm hungry again." Parlay turned to exit the room. "Jessica," he called out. His smooth deep baritone made the sound of her name as interesting as a foreign language.

"Huh?" She stopped what she was doing and peered into his direction.

"I know you 'bout to go and do you." He paused. "Don't let me beat you home." He stood there for a few seconds longer in case she wanted to protest, but she said nothing.

"I be so sick of you niggas, y'all contradicting
I be so bored with myself, can you come and fuck me?
I feel so ordinary, sad when you around me
Treat me like corduroy, wear me out
Arguments, you air me out
Trippin' 'bout your whereabouts
I can't keep no conflict with you
Boy, can we just rub it out..."

Jessica and Diamond cruised the streets, singing along snapping and swaying to the Sza lyrics. Presently, neither of the women could relate, but the tune was so catchy you couldn't help but to sing along. The loud purr from Jessica's Porsche Panamera ripped through the airwaves as she veered onto the freeway.

"It's the next exit!" Diamond yelled over the loud music, pointing forward. Jessica kept snapping. She thought about the words of Diamond. There was no way another man could make her feel half as good as Parlay did. Or could he?

"This it," Diamond spoke in a low tone as the song faded out.

"Hell nah. You see those lights?" Jessica asked, her brows

dipping in confusion. She didn't know what was occurring or what has occurred, but she sure as hell wasn't going to find out. A few police cars were parked outside the club.

"Damn!" Diamond blurted, slapping her thigh. "Okay, look, drive past it and make a left at the light we'll just go to the strip club.

Jessica smacked her lips. "That wasn't a part of the plan. You lucky I like strip clubs," Jessica said while following the directions Diamond had given her.

"Don't trip. It's a whole lotta niggas in there too!"

Jessica and Diamond hopped out the Porsche looking like two video vixens. The five inch stilettoes made her legs and ass look perfect in the "come fuck me dress" that hugged her curves intimately. Diamond's long, blonde human lace flowed gracefully down her back, stopping slightly underneath her ass cheeks. Jessica hair was pinned up in a side ponytail that started at the top of her head and fell close to the center of ribs. Her baby hairs were on fleek, and the brown wavy hair completed her look. Their heels clacked as they made their way to the entry. Women glared, and the men stared. It didn't bother them any as they stood in the extremely short skip line.

"Just give me twenty," the bouncer mumbled.

Without any further questions they did just that and handed it to him. He turned around and looked at their asses as they bypassed him and walked inside.

"Hell nawl, bruh, you told me a hundred!"

"I said it and I meant it, nigga!" the bouncer shot back.

Jessica and Diamond peered over their shoulders and laughed at the situation that soon emerged, then proceed further inside.

"I've been to Tigers Cabaret before, but never this one," Jessica said as they strutted to the bar.

"I like this one better than Tigers," Diamond admitted, squeezing past the small crowd by the bar.

Jessica peered around curiously. She was as eager as Diamond to find out if a man other than her husband had the ability to soak the seat of her panties.

They watched the Hispanic chick mix and match drinks like a professional. Their mouths watered at the sight of the multi-colored alcohol beverages.

"Um——"

"Aye, Leah, let me get a short glass of Henny, no ice, and a hurricane."

Diamond and Jessica peered at the chick in disbelief. "Damn, that was rude!"

Jah was oblivious to their glares until her eyes met theirs. "I cut y'all?" Jah asked. Her brows furrowed.

"Uh, yeah!" they responded in unison.

Jah held up her hands in surrender. "Damn, my bad. My mind in several different places. Leah, get them whatever they want. Put it on my tab," Jah said as she locked eyes with Jessica for the first time. She forgot to blink, not wanting to miss a second of gazing at the beauty that stood before her. Her mouth forgot how to speak.

"Jah!" Leah screamed.

Shamefully, Jah looked from Diamond to Jessica, then Leah, and retrieved the drinks from the bar.

"I'm Jah," she introduced with her free hand.

"Heeey Jah," Diamond responded, a little too friendly.

Jah had seen Diamond before but couldn't place the setting - not at the moment, anyway.

"I'm good," Jessica voiced. There wasn't a reason for introduction because she was too grown for new friends.

Jah placed her hand in her pocket and pulled out a fifty-dollar bill. "Here, Leah. That should cover this and their stuff. This all I'm drinking tonight. You can keep the change."

Leah grinned as Jah walked in the opposite direction.

"Your ass so rude," Diamond said, leaning against the bar.

"So? Bitch, I'm not gay. What is there to talk about?" Jessica shrugged and rolled her eyes.

"Fuck all of that." Diamond waved. "Let's get a li'l liquor in our system."

Jessica sighed in relief as soon as her ass hit the cushion. More people had come jaunting up into the club. A number of men had approached her, but none of them was the kind of men she would even take a second look at. Diamond was being her usual homo-self, receiving lap dances from different strippers. Jessica was already eager to call it a night so that she could be ready and waiting on her man. She took a sip from her drink.

"Excuse me, Ms. Lady."

Jessica peered up and the two of them locked eyes. He was handsome and neatly cut as he hovered over her, smoothing out his beard. He had a natural loud presence in the room even though his voice was low, close to a whisper. His jewelry wasn't flashy: one chain, one ring that adorned his pinky, and a bracelet so massive it looked as if it weighed down his big, bulky arms. He wasn't fat, but he was tall and solid. He was clad in Burberry from head to toe. Sad to say, but Jessica was impressed. His cologne captured Jessica instantly.

"How you doing? I'm Blue." He extended his hand.

The tone in his voice gave her chills, making her hesitant. He gazed into Jessica eyes, never breaking the stare. The VV's in his mouth glistened, and that fluttery feeling surfaced. Although it was just one time, she felt it beat. Yes, her pussy throbbed. That was all the confirmation Jessica needed. She thought of a way to quickly dismiss him. He was too charming. A guy like him would surely get her into some trouble.

"I'm sorry, but I'm married, Blue. It was nice meeting you though," she said with her drink close to her lips.

He licked his lips and grabbed Jessica by the free hand. "It was nice meeting you too." He lifted her hand and kissed the top. His thick lips were so soft for a second she had to close her eyes. He placed it down by her side and headed back into the direction he had come from.

"I guess you were right," Jessica said as soon as she and Diamond locked eyes.

"I told you, bitch! I knew your pussy wasn't broke."

"I never said it was!" Jessica yelled before bursting out in laughter. Her smile faded and she cringed at the way Jah's stare worked knots in her stomach. She turned her head to get away from the intensity in Jah's eyes. However, she cut them in her direction once more upon seeing her make her way towards the exit.

Although Jessica was intrigued by the pole tricks and the dance moves, it was time to go. Her head was hurting and so were her feet. She hated she had to ruin her friend's fun, but if she was that bothered, she could return on her own terms. Every five minutes there was a different ass in her face and Diamond seemed to be enjoying every minute of it.

Jessica was tipsy and feeling good. All she needed was some good dick, but she wouldn't dare get her hopes up. It was nearly two years since the death of Parlay's family, the beginning of his pill addiction, and the end of her perfect relationship.

"Come on, chick, I know you ready to go," Diamond said as she stood slowly to her feet, then tossed her hair over her shoulders. Diamond staggered a few steps backwards. It was obvious that she had way too much to drink. Jessica stood. It must have been quicker than what she intended. She stood motionless to cease her head from spinning.

"Hold up, bitch, you sure we don't need to call an Uber?" Diamond asked, inspecting her from head to toe.

"I'm good. I just got up too quick."

Jessica slid her arm around Diamonds and they left the club together. Neither one of them was expecting the chilly weather, and they used their free hands as they roughly rubbed their arms to work up some heat. Their heels clacked loudly as they made their way to the car.

"Shit, it's cold!" Diamond yelled.

Jessica's teeth chattered uncontrollably, disabling her speech. She unlocked her doors and lowered her engine once she was in arm's reach of her vehicle.

"Ooooh, bitch, I have to pee," Jessica admitted as she climbed inside of her car. Her hands moved quickly as she altered the temperature. Both of them trembled while blowing hot air into the palms of their hands.

Fuck. She instantly regretted not using the restroom before leaving the club. Jessica sped out of the lot in a hurry. She was drunk, but not toasted. She could perfectly function - at least, that's what she thought. The Sza song played, but this time she wasn't as into it as she had been a few hours ago on her way to the club. She gripped her legs tightly, afraid that if she loosened them, she would piss on herself.

Come on, come on...

Jessica raced down the highway. She was merely two exits from Diamond's place. However, the side of the road was beginning to look more appealing than the toilet seats simply because it was a lot closer.

Woop! Woop!

"Hell nah! You must be kidding me." Jessica's palm connected with the steering wheel, instantly awakening Diamond from her slumber. Her heart raced rapidly upon seeing the flashing lights. "Shit!" she whispered as she cleaned the drool from the corner of her mouth. Jessica winced. She knew shit was about to get ugly. She pulled over, smoothed the wrinkles that weren't there, and grabbed a piece of gum out of her cup holder and tossed it inside of her mouth.

It still was not enough. It only took something as simple as the breathalyzer he held in his hand to expose her true, drunken state.

They were both arrested because Diamond had a warrant for unpaid traffic tickets. Jessica was charged with a felony D.W.I.

Chapter 6
Love Don't Love Nobody

Jah's lips brushed Monique's and they weren't even kissing. Her breath heated her face unintentionally as she gaze into Monique's eyes. Jah's mouth moved to her neck, kissing, sucking, and nibbling all in the same spot. This drove Monique wild. It always did. She moaned, then Jah moaned. Jah could feel the moisten between her legs. There was something about Monique that aroused her in the worst way. She loved the faces Monique made, how her body reacted, and even the sounds. Jah's hands quickly slid between the folds of Monique's silk robe. There was nothing underneath. She grazed her hand across the top of her shaven pussy. Monique's back arched off the bed. "Oooohhh," she cooed. Jah knew exactly where and how to touch her.

"Damn, you so wet." Overwhelmingly aroused, Jah slipped two fingers inside of her, longing to get a feel. Her thumb remained outside. Constant moans and pleading fell from her lips as Jah slowly rotated her thumb around, across, and over her swollen button. She leaned down and kissed Monique, muffling her cries. Her body trembled beneath her hand. The orgasm lasted unusually long. It was so intense she was afraid to let go of Jah once it was over. She didn't want her to move. She wanted to fall asleep in the position they were in.

After a few moments, Jah slowly slid her fingers out and put them in her mouth with a grin. She leaned forward and kissed her on the forehead. "Get you some sleep, bae."

Jah may have wanted more and she could tell Monique did too, but since their schedules were completely different most days, it was only right she get the rest she deserved. Monique was an RN at the VA. She worked twelve-hour shifts four days a week. Her hours were seven to seven. She made it home, cooked and showered, then took a nap. She managed to wake up minutes before midnight as well as minutes before Jah arrived. She needed her fix. Without it she wouldn't be able to sleep peacefully. She was an addict, and Jah was her drug.

Jah watched Monique's chest rise and fall as she lay on her side, sound asleep. She walked into the kitchen and warmed the plate Monique had cooked for her. Seeing Monique's screen light up, Jah reached for her phone. Her brows furrowed. The number was unfamiliar, but the text wasn't. It was the way the person misspelled the common words that grabbed Jah's attention. She tapped the screen, entering the text history. Her heart was pounding in her chest as she debated mentally. She slammed the door to the refrigerator shut and dropped Monique's phone on the counter. Her fists were clenched as she stalked toward the bedroom, but like a bulb, something went off in her head and she quickly reconsidered. She popped her knuckles as she let out quick short breaths in an attempt to calm herself down.

The microwave sounded. The food was done, and so was her appetite. She left that food behind and flopped down on the sofa.

Jah started shaking her head, trying to shake off the dark thoughts that were swarming in her head. A single tear slid down her hardened face as she sat in the darkness alone. Monique was her earth, her peace. This news was surely unexpected, and if someone would've told her instead of her seeing it, she wouldn't have wasted a second considering it. However, she'd seen it with her own eyes, an image that would be embedded in her memory forever.

Chapter 7
Who Can I Run To

Parlay nodded off as he sat in the loveseat beside the window, awaiting Jessica's return. Anger coupled with disappointment as he racked his brain as to her whereabouts. He grabbed his phone off the coffee table in front of him.

2:41 a.m.

He shook his head slowly in disbelief. This wasn't like Jessica. She wasn't the type to simply buck the system. Whenever given a directive, she followed it.

Ring! Ring! Ring!

He quickly answered the phone, hoping it'd be the answer to his question.

"You have a collect call from——"

Parlay answered before he even heard the name. It had to be her. He knew, he felt, that it was her.

"Hello?"

"Lay, baby! Look, I just got booked in. I've been here hours already. They pulled me over coming from the club for driving while intoxicated."

"Hang tight. I'm on my way. When you make it upstairs, call me collect."

The operator came in shortly after and the free sixty second call ended immediately.

Parlay sighed deeply, searching through his phone for Luther's number. Luther was his attorney, whom he kept on standby. Even though he moved with caution, in his line of profession, you never knew when a situation would arise. Parlay stayed ready to keep getting ready. He pressed the phone against his ear, waiting to hear Luther on the other end.

"Hello?" he mumbled, evidently awakened from a deep slumber.

"Luther, I need you."

***

Parlay sat across from Luther at his desk.

"Okay, that's everything, I faxed everything to the jail. It's going to take the paperwork a few hours to process and she'll be back on the streets."

A genuine smile etched Parlay's face as he stuck out his hand. He deeply sighed in relief. "Man, I 'preciate you, bruh."

"No need to thank me. You pay me enough," Luther responded, expressing the same gratitude.

Parlay rushed out of the building. If he moved quickly, he still had time to meet with his therapist. Unbeknownst to Jessica, Parlay had started the therapy sessions after realizing the medication wasn't good enough.

Parlay laid comfortably on a brown suede couch, intensely staring at the ceiling. Dr. Haskins spoke clear English, but with a heavy Haitian accent. Her skin was unusually dark - so dark she almost looked purple - but she was beautiful. Her eyes were hazel, which he found odd and surprising. Although, Dr. Haskins was highly spiritual, she had a way of making people feel comfortable with her. She had a special skill for making people open up to her. His head was slightly propped up by a small pillow.

The room was quiet with the exception of Dr. Haskins clicking her pen seldomly. A subtle smell of vanilla lingered around. She sat in a corner with a notepad in hand, studying Parlay's every move.

"She was going to tell me, I felt it, but I guess after everything happened, she changed her mind. She thought I was..." Parlay spoke in a low tone before pausing. Gruesome images invaded his mental. He squeezed his eyes shut and just as he hoped, they went away. They always did - temporarily. He took a deep breath, cleared his throat, and clenched his jaw firmly. He was trying his damndest to fight off tears as he took a hard swallow. He inhaled deeply and slowly exhaled, almost as if he could uncage some of the pain that was built up by simply blowing it out. He closed his eyes and started to speak again. "She thought I was crazy, and the shit bothers me as deeply as the loss of my family. That was my family as well." As he lay back, a single tear slipped down his face, traveling down to the tip of his ear. Parlay quickly jerked forward.

"I'm listening," Doctor Haskins said. Her natural coils and kinky hair was pulled neatly into a tight bun on top of her head. Parlay was so contrary and mysterious. He was a man she couldn't quite understand. She was intrigued, but she would never tell him that. "Continue," she said eagerly, wanting him to finish. Still, no response. She had been seeing him for months, and he never revealed who this "her" was. She knew the woman, whoever she was, was partially responsible for his pain, but he never talked about her for more than a few sentences. Indeed, there was progression. She wanted to hear more.

He remained quiet appearing to be in deep thought.

"I can't. All I see is…" his voice began to fade. "What could've been," Parlay admitted as he shook his head in grief.

"I know it's heart-wrenching to lose family——" the doctor said.

But before she could finish her sentence, Parlay stood up and grabbed his hoodie. "My bad, Doc. I have to run," he said as he gave her a forced grin. "'Preciate ya though."

"That's fine. I'll see you next week, right?" Dr. Haskins asked as she smiled back with her genuine eyes.

"For sho' I'll be back, and I'll be on time too," Parlay said just before exiting her office.

In the ten years she had been practicing, she had never had a patient so evasive and so hard to crack open. Parlay had been coming for eight months straight, and their sessions never lasted thirty minutes. He would start and suddenly leave. It never failed. But today, things were different. He was a bit more detailed and he spoke longer than usual. Dr. Haskins was finally making progress.

Little did she know, he hadn't spoken to anyone about the particular events or the ones leading up to that day. Since she was a complete stranger, she should consider herself lucky. She was the only one, and Parlay planned to keep it that way. He was indeed coming next week, and the week after. Although he didn't say much, there was a lot to him, a lot that needed to be freed, and the only chance to do so was with Doctor Haskins.

Chapter 8
Everything's Out in the Open

"Polo!" Jah yelled into the crowd huddled around the entry of the barbershop.

They paid little attention to the TV as it displayed the fighters' highlights. They were too busy placing their bets.

"Come on." Jah waved him over. "You the last one for today."

"Aww, man!"

"Man, come on, li'l Jah."

"Fam, I'm about to go see my bitch."

Different voices called out, displeased with her decision.

"Shit, I'm trying to do the same. I been up here for damn near ten hours," Jah claimed.

A few of them smacked their lips. Most of them walked out. Gambling may have been their focus, but getting faded was their main priority.

"Come fuck with me tomorrow. I got y'all." She paused. "I'm tired, man." Jah wasn't tired in a physical sense, but mentally and emotionally, she was beat. Those texts and images she had seen in Monique's phone last night had haunted her mental non-stop. She knew work would be the perfect distraction, and it was, but not like she planned. She was hurting, like a thorn in her flesh. It was a constant pain. She knew the cause of it, where it stemmed from. She just didn't know how to stop it.

"Are you dressed?" Jah texted Monique. She had called her nearly an hour ago and told her to look her best. Tonight, they'd be celebrating a special occasion and she needed to be the baddest bitch in the room. Instead of responding with a text, Monique responded with a picture.

A nasty taste filled Jah's mouth. Indeed, she was gorgeous. But she was a deceitful, lying-ass bitch too, and because of her disloyalty, she despised her. On top of all of that, Jah still had to make it back in time to attend her drug class. It was part of her deferred probation. She only had eight classes left, and once they were complete, her probation would be also.

It took Jah another fifteen minutes to finish. She cleaned up her booth and left. She was anxious to make it to Monique. She was hurt. True enough, she did her thing - seldomly and nothing in comparison to the thing she did with Monique. Jah could see the messages every time she closed her eyes. The thought alone sent her into a rage. She blinked rapidly, fighting back tears of anger because of Monique and tears of hurt because of herself. There was no one to blame but herself for falling and being real in the midst of it.

Jah used the back of her hand to remove any proof of the truth. There was no point in expressing how she felt because Monique didn't care anyways. If she did, she wouldn't be sitting in her car thinking of a way to body a bitch without getting caught. Killing Monique would only satisfy her for so long. Slow torture was the best revenge. If you're dead, you can't feel, and she wanted Monique to feel exactly the way she felt, but worse. Jah peered back at her reflection through the rearview mirror. Anyone with eyes could look at her and see that she was in a world of pain.

Honk! Honk!

There was no point of getting out and getting dressed. She was ready to address the situation. Shortly, Monique came strutting out of their apartment and down the steps. She lifted her large, beachy straw hat and she paused and grabbed it before it ran away from her. A little cleavage was exposed, displaying her small paw prints. The dress didn't hug her body, but her curves were still very noticeable. Jah clenched her jaws tight as she gripped the steering wheel. Seeing her at her best angered Jah even more. Any other day, Jah relished Monique's beauty, because she belonged to her.

However, she didn't find anything attractive about a female that belonged to everybody.

"Hey baby," Monique greeted in a cheesy voice as she stepped inside.

Bitch.

The first thing Jah spotted was her perfectly-pedicured toes. They were white, complementing her wedge heels. She knew Jah loved it when she painted her toes white. She shifted uncomfortably in her seat as she highly considered killing the bitch.

"Hey," Jah spoke back then forced a grin. Pretending to be okay was as difficult as facing her fears.

Monique sighed deeply. Her eyes gleamed with joy. She was a sucker for surprises. Only this time, she wouldn't find this one so thrilling. She crossed her legs at her ankles. "Sooo, bae, where we going?"

Jah cringed as soon as the word "bae" fell from her lying lips. "You'll see," Jah replied.

"I want to know! Tell me, bae," Monique begged.

Jah decided to give her a few hints since she was so curious, seeing if Monique would remember any of the texts sent or received. Jah decided to use Monique's conversation to clue in on their destination.

"You miss me?" Jah asked, her eyes never leaving the road.

"Of course, bae, I always miss you," she responded in a chill tone.

Jah nodded. "Whenever we get back, you think you can make me your famous chicken and dumplings?" she asked, her eyes still glued to the road, afraid to look Monique in the eyes because doing so would easily expose every emotion she had bottled inside.

"Of course, bae!"

Jah was listening for any hesitation, but there wasn't any. Since she didn't sense her sarcasm, she continued on.

"Cool, and after that, I want you to put on that red teddy and dance for me."

"O-okay."

Jah's heart was pounding in her chest. *Yeah, bitch, I'm on to that ass. You can lie all you want.* Jah got quiet she want her mind to wander. Monique tried masking it, but it was too late. Her hesitation spoke volumes.

"What song you want me to throw on, that Megan Thee Stallion and twerk for you?" The chick that she had been texting did indeed specify the song. Jah figured if she said that, it would be a dead giveaway. She wasn't ready to expose her hand just yet - not until she got closer to her destination.

"I'll let you know."

Minutes passed, and not even a word had been uttered from either of them. A text came through Monique's phone and Jah quickly cut her eyes in that direction.

Shiesty bitch.

Jah happened to catch her open and delete the message. She couldn't believe how close Monique was playing her, and with her ex-lover, at that. They say it's not good to leave the one you love for the one you like. Since Monique was the one that had gotten left, Jah didn't think to take heed.

She should have. Like most humans, Monique simply couldn't get rid of her past. In spite of all the detriment the chick caused her, her inability to cut ties with her past cost a great future. Jah would've gone to the moon and back for her. She always made her feel like she was the only woman in the world, even though she was just the only woman for her. She never put her in any drama because she never led a bitch on. She was simply as close to perfect as prefect gets. Needless to say, her good still wasn't good enough.

Directions spewed from the GPS. They were only three minutes from their destination. Jah spotted a little movement out of the corner of her eye. She cut her eyes in Monique's direction. Her brows dipped as her curiosity heightens.

"Jah, where are we going?" Monique said in a whisper tone, her voice barely audible. If Jah wouldn't have been so focused on any slight movement indicating her guilt, she wouldn't have heard her. She did though.

"I told you, we going where you want to go. You been trying for weeks now, so I'm taking you."

Monique racked her brain. She was no longer reclined in her seat at ease. She was sitting stiffly up straight, her back inches away from the leather seat as she zoned in on the road ahead. For the first time since getting inside of Jah's car, she dreaded their destination. She turned to face Jah.

"Jah, take me back home. Wherever it is you're taking me, I don't want to go."

"Come to think of it, I think I know the song I want you to dance to," she responded, completely ignoring her request. She was less than two miles away from her destination.

"We can talk about that at the apartment." Monique crossed her arms over her chest.

"Turn left on Cove Street," the operation announced.

"Sex With You," Jah said.

Monique gasped sharply. Her heart banged in her chest. Jah's comment was confirmation. It was the same song Ray had chosen. Ray was Monique's ex-lover. Perplexion pairing with shame, Monique gently grabbed Jah's forearm, the same arm Jah used to steer with. Jah was so withdrawn she never heard anything Monique said, nor did she feel her fidgety hand against her skin.

"Please stop," Monique said, choking on her tears. They were getting close. Ray's Nissan Altima was now in view. Monique grip tightened as she dug her nails into her flesh.

"Stop!" she yelled, petrified. Black liquid streamed down her face, a mixture of her mascara and tears. Her once-beat face that she spent nearly an hour perfecting was destroyed within a matter of seconds. Now they were directly across the street. Panicky and flustered, Monique began yelling all sorts of obscenities.

For the first time, Jah turned in her seat and locked eyes with Monique. Her eyes were as numb as her heart as she stared at Monique with an icy glare. Monique paused in apprehension. She sat there motionless, afraid of the unfamiliar eyes that stared back at her.

"You and this bitch been plotting to meet up for weeks now." Her lips were tight, forming a small circle.

"Can we please go home and talk about this?" She reached over in an attempt to console Jah.

Jah pushed her hand away with force. "Get out." The vacancy in Jah's eyes were as empty as her stomach since she hadn't eaten one single thing since finding the evidence.

"No, I don't want to get out. I don't want to be here!" Her voice was full of emotions, a ball of emotions that longed to be free, but they were stuck. Stuck in the center of her chest, blocking her wind pipe, making it hard for her to breath. Monique felt cornered.

Jah pulled her phone out. Monique watched her as she swallowed the lump in her throat, dreading what Jah would do next. She was calling someone. She wondered who Jah could possibly be calling at a time like this. At that instant, it dawned on her. She reached out in attempt to get rid of the phone that was pressed against Jah's ear. Jah gripped her fingers, breaking two of her freshly-manicured nails.

"Ouch, Jah! You're hurting me!" Monique winced.

Jah bent her fingers backwards, forcing Monique to arch her back in pain. She glared at her the entire time, secretly enjoying the pain she was implementing.

A voice came through the other end.

"Aye, come outside and get ya bitch, bro," Jah said without loosening her grip.

Ray placed a hand over her free ear as she spoke loudly into the receiver. With Monique hollering at the top of her lungs, it made it difficult for her to hear.

"Who is this?" Ray didn't want to speak too loudly and alert her fiancée, who was asleep in the bedroom.

"You heard what I said. You and this bitch been trying to hook up. Well, here she go." Jah ended the call and released the grip on Monique fingers. Swiftly, she reached over and opened and forcefully pushed the passenger door open.

"Get out," Jah demanded again.

Monique sat there frozen, certainly stunned. She had never witnessed this side of Jah. Remorse filled her instead as if it was poured into her. Her lips began to tremble. "I'm sorry, Jah." She gently covered Jah's hand with hers.

Jah chewed the inside of her lip as she blankly studied the person responsible for her unhappiness. "Get out." Her voice as steady as her eyes. Monique slid her hand up and down Jah's apologetically. Jah snatched her hand away and shoved Monique forcefully. Monique's body jerked to the right, her head snapping on impact.

"Jah!" she yelled hastily, gripping the ledge on the inside of the door to prevent herself from hitting the cement.

Jah shoved and Monique continued to hold on. Finished with the back and forth, Jah leaned back in her seat until her body was pressed against the window. She lifted her Timberland boot and with all of her might, she kicked Monique in the midsection. Monique's grip loosened as she gasped sharply. "Jah! Stop!" Frightened and panicky, Monique continued to yell at the top of her lungs. She reached back and kicked again, and this time her foot connected with Monique's side. She lowered her leg a bit and forcefully, but slowly, mashed forward. Monique's ass hit the pavement, followed by a loud thud. Jah scrambled hastily to close the door before she had the chance to get back inside. Her wet palms stuck to the glass as she leaned against the car, begging for Jah's mercy. Jah's chest heaved as she did all she could to calm down and control her breathing. She was amped. She would have never thought she and Monique would be at a place like this.

Jah always thought she and Monique would wed and grow old together. So much for that. She opened the driver's door and stood slightly outside of her car.

"Don't worry about coming to pick up your shit. I'm packing it and taking it to your mama's house."

And with that, Jah left. She didn't know, or care to know, how Monique would get to her mom's, but she was certain that she would find a way.

Chapter 9
Don't Knock It Til You Try It

Jessica's heels clacked against the marble tile as she headed inside the room. She sighed deeply before pushing the door open, stepping inside. She peered around the room, annoyed, glancing at each unfamiliar face in the room. She rolled her eyes self-consciously, then headed in the direction of the sign-in sheet.

Fucking around with Diamond's ass, now I have to deal with this bullshit. One of Jessica's stipulations upon her release was to attend a substance treatment class for eight weeks, one class per week. Her smug expression was clear to everyone else how she felt about the class.

Unbeknownst to Jessica, Jah sat in the corner of the room, her usual spot. She participated in the group, but just enough. She wasn't an over achiever, nor was she a nonparticipant. Jah was somewhere in between the two.

The pace of her heart increased as soon as she spotted the beauty from the club last night. Jessica's was a face she'd never forget because her beauty captivated her like no other. Her walk was as mesmerizing as her beauty. Jah sat comfortably with her legs gapped open, discreetly watching Jessica from across the room. Her fitted was pulled down low over her eyebrows, nearly coving her eyes. However, Jah could see clearly. Jessica hadn't noticed her yet, and truthfully, Jah didn't want her to. She was going to pretend to act just as uninterested as she was.

After signing the sign-in sheet, Jessica grabbed a chair. The men and women seated in the circle scooped in separate directions to make room for her.

Jessica scowled at some of the poorly-dressed people seated inside the circle. Reluctantly, she took a seat, crossing her legs and clutching her bag against her midsection, acting as if she was some sort of germophobe. It was odd that Jessica behaved so uptight around such people, when she was raised by people of their kind.

Jessica's mother and father were both addicts, but their addictions differed. Her father was addicted to money. He would do any and everything for a dollar. Lucky for him, he didn't have to do anything degrading, at least. With his endless love for money and charming gift of gab, he became one of the most notorious pimps in Dallas. However, his empire crashed and burned nearly a decade after it started. He was arrested on multiple trafficking, pimping and pandering charges. Ultimately, he was sentenced to prison for twenty-eight years when Jessica was just seven years old.

Her mother was an addict as well, and although there were similarities in their addictions, there was differences also. Jessica's mother was addicted to love. She never knew the feeling she desperately yearned for. Upon meeting Jessica's father, she never felt so unique and relevant. She became obsessed with him and the way he tugged at her heartstrings. She wanted nothing more. She needed it as if it was a basic necessity, as if it was as significant as water, food and shelter. She fell in love with him and he fell in love with the lifestyle and what she contributed to it.

A little after Jessica's father was imprisoned, her mother had driven six hours to visit him in Amarillo, TX at Clements Unit. A hating-ass guard gave her some news that nearly busted one of the veins in her heart. The day her mother appeared at the prison, her father happen to be in visitation. It pained her when she learned, and she even had opportunity of peeking inside on the ceremony. She had been a team member since she could remember, but she always held the lead position. There was a new HBIC, and she didn't like the image or idea one bit. She left in a hurry. The strength she thought she had dissipated before she even made it home.

Luckily, she did make it home. Perhaps she should've gone someplace else instead. She wasn't able to control the emotions that engulfed her as soon as she walked inside the exact place they shared for years. Memories surfaced, both beautiful and ugly. Humiliation coupled with rejection left her mother in a trapped state of mind.

There was only one way to numb the pain. She decided to numb it with even more pain, but the pain lasted merely a few seconds until she couldn't feel anymore, see anything, or breathe. The blade hit the cement, bloody as the wrist she sliced open. She bled out, leaving Jessica to fend for herself in this world.

Jessica's grandmother took her and Diamond in. Her grandmother was like most older black women, the ones born in the fifties and sixties, unsparing and attentive simply because they were raised in such a modest and hospitable environment. However, because her grandmother loved those who were quite eccentric, she found herself surrounded by those very same people. The crazy thing is, the majority of them were family members. The strays that would spend nights were close friends of her cousins. Jessica had four male cousins. They all suffered from severe drug addictions. They were the usual definition of strung out. Jessica's grandmother did everything in her power to keep Jessica away from her tainted cousins. Unbeknownst to the grandmother, they did everything in their power to keep Jessica away from them. Jessica was as pestering as a quarrelsome wife, and the last thing they needed was her around blowing their high.

This place reminded her of her cousins, but she behaved like she was as accustomed as they were. Still clutching her bag as if someone would snatch it and run, she surveyed every face in the room. Some she scanned quicker than most. However, when her eyes locked with the set of eyes across the room, something happened, perhaps, a slight flutter in her chest, perhaps change in her breathing. She couldn't tell, and surely no one else could. She swallowed the baby lump in her throat. She shifted in her seat uncomfortably, pulling her hair behind her ear.

Jah sensed her uneasiness immediately. Jessica grimaced, feeling completely exposed. A half smile slowly etched Jah's face as she glorified in Jessica's discomfort.

"Good evening, ladies. Welcome to NA/AA. My name is Bella, and I'll be your facilitator tonight." She smiled. It was chilled, but she was cute, so it didn't look too bad.

"Good evening, Bella," everyone said in unison.

"Hey, I'm Tesla, and I'm a recovering addict."

Each person around the circle continued to share their name and their personal business. Jessica's nostrils flared. Her agitation was evident.

I'm not admitting I'm an addict. I'm not a damn addict.

Bella, the facilitator, nodded her head in Jessica's direction. It was her turn to introduce herself to the others. Jessica swiveled from left to right, pretending to be oblivious to what was occurring. She sighed deeply. "I'm Jessica," she responded quickly. She clutched her bag even tighter. Bella was still looking at her, grinning.

"You have to say you're a recovering addict," Misty voiced. Misty was one of the women in the circle.

Bella shot Misty a disappointing look. One of the rules during the meeting was "no blurting out."

"I'm not saying that. Now move along," Jessica stated. Her tone was firm and unyielding.

Jah chuckled. She had done the same exact thing her first day, and soon found out how something that simple affected her successfully completing the class.

What went by quickly to them seemed to drag by to Jessica. Jah was so consumed with her thoughts that time flew by for her as well.

"Ladies, it's time for your ten-minute break," Bella announced.

Jah didn't move. Jessica flew to her feet and out the door. She dashed inside of the restroom and towards the nearest stall. She pulled her phone out of her bra and locked the stall all at once.

"Hey you," Parlay answered.

"Baby, this class sucks ass. I don't know how I'm going to make it through the next seven," Jessica complained, sitting fully dressed on the toilet seat.

"You'll be alright. It's either that or back to the county jail," he said, followed by a slight chuckle.

"That's not funny. I'll be home in an hour. You want me to grab you something to eat?"

"I got a taste for pizza. I'm leaving later on. Me and Prime heading to the A so we can make it back by tomorrow evening."

Jessica signed deeply. It was something she did every time Parlay mentioned a drop. Even though it was never longer than a day's time, it was still quite disturbing. "Okay. I'll call you when I get out of class."

Parlay could detect the exasperation in her tone. She was going to either be with a broke nigga who could give her all the time she craved and nothing to go with it, or a nigga that couldn't give her the time she hoped for, but the world and everything in it. The choice was hers, and Jessica had already made her decision. She was a woman with expensive taste.

After ending the call, Jessica retreated back to the classroom. She dragged. It was clear that she was in no hurry.

Everyone was lined up around the table once Jessica entered the room. Coffee and a subtle vanilla scent lingered though out the room. Boxes of fresh, warm pastries were neatly stacked in the middle of the table. Her mouth watered. A cup of coffee would be nice.

Jah sucked the glaze off her finger as she noticed Jessica step back inside. She eased over to the circle, where Jessica sat alone.

"You want some coffee?" Jah asked, hovering over her from behind.

Jessica turned around just enough to see who she was. Jah held the cup of iced coffee out, hoping she would take it.

Jessica scowled in disgust. She turned back around. "I'm good, and I definitely wouldn't want to drink after you, I don't know where your mouth been."

Jah was a bit appalled by her bluntness. Her lips turned downwards as she nodded her head slowly. Jah turned to walk away, but stopped misstep.

"Aye, what I really came to tell you was that you should consider participating, because if it gets back to the counselor that you're not, they can extend your length of classes." She walked away.

Curious, Jessica turned around in her seat, but Jah had already walked away. The last thing she wanted was to stay longer than what she intended. As much as the silly greeting went against everything she stood for, she would have to simply put her pride to the side and play by the rules.

Chapter 10
Let's Go to the A

Parlay covered his ears and squeezed his eyes shut as he tried muffling the constant cries that mentally disturbed his peace morning, noon, and night. The blaring and unharmonious cries made casual conversation impossible. Some days were easier than others. However, the effect of the Xanax ceased the clamor and the gruesome images. As hard as Parlay tried to desert the addictive pill, he couldn't. It was more beneficial than detrimental, in his eyes.

Usually, Prime and Parlay made two trips a month to Atlanta. However, business was better than it had ever been, so the men planned a trip a week sooner than usual. Parlay threw back a few aspirin afterwards. He had a pestering migraine that made him want to climb back into his California king-sized bed and sleep until the next day. On top of the migraine, Parlay felt drained. He wasn't sure if it was mentally, physically, or emotionally drained. Perhaps all three.

The night Jessica went out perturbed his mental. However, he would never tell her or anyone else that. Maybe his therapist, if the topic emerged. Parlay wasn't the jealous type, and he was well aware of the close relationship she and Diamond possessed. However, he wasn't witless to the signs. In the years of him and Jessica dating, she rarely had girls' night out. She did in the beginning, but after a year or so, she invited Parley to every occasion, altering the initial event. She had a few associates, but Diamond was really the only friend. Everyone thought they were sisters because that's what they would tell people, but Parlay knew the facts. Whenever the two would hook up, it was during the day, only at night if Jessica was going to Diamond's place or vice versa. But a club?

Parlay wanted to interrogate her until he was free from the emotional or mental agitation, but he opted against it, afraid that he'd sound like a bitch. His father had taught him to deal with his own issues because others weren't going to care to. Because of that, Parlay swept a lot of shit under the rug. However, his rug looked more like a mattress with everything he had stuff underneath. Unbeknownst to Dr. Haskins, her sessions were one of the best things that happened to Parlay.

There was the sound of keys, then he heard her heels clack against the tile. Jessica had made it. He ran his hand down his face and headed towards the kitchen. The loud tomato and garlic aroma lit up the house within seconds, forcing Parlay to rub his stomach.

"Hey bae." He walked up behind her, burying his head in her neck, the smell of mango and peaches instantly assaulting his nostrils.

Jessica smiled and turned around. She placed both hands on his cheeks and kissed his lips. "Hey baby, I missed you," she said, gazing into his eyes. Her smile slowly faded as she noticed the fatigue in his brown irises. "What's wrong?" she asked, concerned.

"I'm just tired, that's all," Parlay answered, masking the truth like always. He pretended to yawn. Jessica couldn't tell that it was fake.

"Go out of town tomorrow then. Get some rest, baby. I'll go for you if you want me to."

"Aww, baby, I'll never ask you to do that. I'm good," he assured slightly lifting her off her feet, planting an abundance of kisses on her lips.

"What time you leaving?"

Parlay peered down at his watch. "In about two hours."

Jessica spun on her heels. "That'll give us time to cuddle."

***

"What yo boy?" Prime asked in a chipper tone.

The two of them slapped hands and Prime did a little dance afterwards. Parlay dragged to the passenger side. He really wasn't in no mood for the trip.

"I'm good. What the fuck you so happy 'bout?" Parlay asked, climbing inside the truck.

Still grinning, Prime pulled his phone out of his pocket, tapped his screen a few times, then turned the screen in his direction. It was one of the prettiest pussies he had ever seen.

Damn. His left brow raised in awe. He turned his mouth downward as he nodded slowly in approval.

"I'm 'bout to go see that thang in person", Prime joked.

Their bodies jerked slightly as he put the car in drive and pulled off. The pack was the last thing they would pick up whenever they were out in the big city. This was solely to avoid any mishaps.

"Aye——" Parlay started but ceased his speech when Natasha's Facebook profile came into view. She had sent him a friend request. A half smile etched his face as he peered at the beautiful woman he once possessed many feelings for. He was about to tell Prime about the time schedule they were on but decided against it.

This trip might not be so bad after all.

His smile immediately turned into a scowl once he realized that he had spoken too soon. Baffled, his brows crimped after seeing the images of her and the guy who appeared to be her husband. That tugged at his heart strings, and he found the feeling quite disturbing. Parlay swallow the lump in his throat as he kept scrolling through her gallery. She looked joyful. After glancing at every picture she had uploaded, he slid his phone in his pocket. He bobbed his head to the Jeezy lyrics, pretending to be unbothered.

"White keys, piano
Detroit, Atlanta

Mac-town, Savannah
White keys, piano
Bitch, I'm Beethoven of the block (yeah)…"

"Hold on, hold on," Prime chimed in, balancing his phone between his and his shoulders as he turned the volume down.

Parlay shook his head at the absurdity. He could tell by Prime's eagerness that the chick he had planned to hook up with was on the other end of the phone. Parlay simply found it quite odd that a woman who lacked such class and self-respect could be so captivating.

Prime hadn't stop talking about the chick since their last visit. Indeed, she was drop dead gorgeous, but outer beauty was plentiful nowadays. A beautiful woman with no morals, principles, or values is just as significant as an ugly female with no ass. She lacked self-discipline, broadcasting her weakness. She had given Prime the pussy and he didn't even know her name, clearly indicating that shorty couldn't be trusted, period.

"What's up, baby? Where you at?"

Parlay couldn't hear her response and he didn't try. He turned his attention to the scenery outside of his window. Prime peered in Parlay's direction and smiled. Parlay wasn't aware of it. The Xanax had him too lax. He needed to eat something so that he could sober up just a little bit. He was familiar with Atlanta and even knew a couple of people. However, that still wasn't enough leverage to allow him to be zooted out of his mind in a city other than his own. Parlay was about to tell Prime to stop somewhere so they could grab a bite to eat when he realized the car had slowed. Parlay peered up at the Letty's Veggies, then peered back at Prime. His eyes filled with uncertainty. Prime grinned boyishly as he unbuckled his seat belt.

"What?" he asked, seeing the intensity in Parlay eyes.

"Why you pick here?" Parlay asked, his tone very serious.

"Whoa." Prime held his hands up. "I thought you'd want to come here. Plus, shorty likes the food here, so this is where we decided to meet up."

A part of Parlay wanted to see Natasha, but the other part felt a little jealous about her marriage and couldn't care less if he saw her or not. However, since they were already there, it left him no options.

Prime immediately spotted his boo thang and bopped in her direction. Parlay stood there his hands stuffed inside of his Amiri jeans.

"Hey." The hostess stared at him through narrow slits and she pointed at him as if it was some kind of tactic to help her remember who he was.

Parlay shot her a look of confusion. He had never seen the chick before. He was certain that she wasn't the chick from last time.

"Damn, I can't remember." She deeply exhaled.

"Remember what?" Parlay looked at her questionably.

"It starts with a P." She snapped her fingers. This was another tactic of hers.

"Parlay," Parlay blurted wrinkles decorating his forehead.

"Yes, yes, that's it. My boss showed all of us a picture of you and she said to notify her immediately if you stop by." She spit out the words as if they were rehearsed, clasping her hands in front of her as she rocked on the balls of her feet.

Her performance forced a smile upon Parlay's face. Instantly, his once cranky mood dissipated. He ran a hand down his face, unable to hide the grin peeking through.

"Have a seat over there." She removed a menu from her apron. "Take this so you can order, I'll be back in a few, I'm going to get my boss." Her high ponytail swayed left to right as she trotted off to go and get Natasha.

Meanwhile, on the other side of the restaurant, Prime and his shorty aimlessly chatted about things that were going on in their lives during the time they spent away from each other. Their food sat in front of them, but they were gazing and talking more than anything.

"So what do they call you around your way?" Prime asked, finally seeking out her name.

"Well, my name is Genesis, but most people call me Gen." Her tight green eyes were as mesmerizing as her full, succulent lips. Her hair was down today. Her blonde hair enhanced her perfectly-toned skin, giving her an exotic touch. She wore little to no makeup; just lashes and deep red lipstick.

Prime couldn't take his eyes off her lips. He always fantasized about getting sucked off by a female with lipstick on. It was the smearing of the lipstick that turned him on. He cleared his throat once he realized that he was so busy staring that he hadn't responded. "That's sexy. Your name fits you."

They locked eyes, each of them conveying their lust for each other.

Genesis twirled a few strands of her hair. "Why you looking at me like that?" she asked in a whispered tone. She traced her lips with her tongue, instantly making the vein in Prime's dick pulsate.

He leaned forward, placing his elbows on the table. "I want to take your sexy ass down."

His eyes were so intense that a course of heat shot from her toes to her head, immediately soiling her panties and hardening her nipples. Genesis had chosen the restaurant so that she and Prime could set aside their burning desire and truly get to know each other. However, those plans faded as soon as he sat across from her. He watched her in the way a man with an obsession would, but in a confident way. He wasn't afraid to deny it and didn't care to hide it. He wanted her and whatever she had to give and was ready to take things she wasn't capable of giving.

"Take me," Genesis said.

"Don't tempt me," Prime shot back, grabbing the crotch of his Nike joggers.

Genesis eased up from the table and walked towards the rear of the restaurant. He couldn't tell where she was going, but he followed. Her walk was magnetic, highlighting her round bubble butt. She veered to the left inside the woman's bathroom. Prime glanced left to right, then entered as well. A subtle lavender scent lingered around the spacious restroom.

Genesis took off towards the last stall, her ass bouncing with every step. Prime was a bit hesitant, knowing Parlay's relationship with the owner, but his fervent urge led him to do it anyways. Genesis was down to just her bra and panties by the time Prime made it.

"Damn, li'l baby," he commented as he approached her.

She unlatched her bra, allowing it to open and slowly fall to the ground. He couldn't stop himself from groping her coconut-sized breasts. They were full and perky. He lowered his lips to her hard nipples and kissed them gently.

"We don't have to rush," she said in spite of the setting.

"I wouldn't call it rushing. Let's just say I'm ready." He yanked his joggers down to his ankles.

She reached out and grabbed his stiff dick. White and gold Fendi briefs hugged his thighs and ass cheeks, his thick pile hardening by the second, threatening to tear the stretchy material. She squatted before him and pulled down his briefs as well. They were now directly on top of his joggers. He stepped one leg out of the clothes, enabling him to do any and everything he wanted to do. He gently toyed with the mushroom tip as he gazed into her tight eyes.

"Go lock the door," he ordered, and she wasted no time doing so. He never took his eyes off her. Prime thought he'd bust just from the idea of bussin'.

She ran towards him, her perky breasts bouncing in the process. Her lace thong covered the hidden treasure that he was dying to unveil. She wrapped her arms around his neck, slightly jumping off the ground. Her soft breasts pressed against his chest as he lifted her up by her plump ass. She wrapped her legs around his midsection dampening his torso. The feel of her wetness drove Prime into a frenzy. He moved towards the sink and placed her on top of it. He cupped her face roughly and pressed his lips against hers. They shared the same amount of passion as they explored each other's mouths. He covered her bottom lip, tugged on it, and sucked it before releasing it. She did the same. They ended their passionate kiss with a soft peck. They gazed into each other's eyes like they had just exchanged vows, their chests heaving. Without moving anything but his eyes, he focused on her lace undies.

"Pull 'em to the side," Prime ordered.

Genesis's hand trembled as she found her way to the underwear. Her hand wasn't the only thing that trembled. Her heart and soul did as well. A man she had only known two weeks had captivated her in every way possible, rattling things inwardly that she thought didn't exist. His meaty dick tapped at her opening.

Itty bitty nigga, but his dick big.

Two thick veins ran from the base to the tip. She eyed it like a recovering addict who was about to relapse. He moved two hands around her honeypot. She was super wet and sticky. Without warning he tore through her walls and fell into her tunnel.

"Shit!" she yelped in pain, arching her back.

He pulled completely out and fell back in. He rolled and grinded inside of her with patience and precision.

"This shit hurt so fucking good," she admitted breathlessly after biting him in his shoulder. She dug her stilettos nails into his back as he pumped in and out of her.

Prime knew he was about to buss. He wasn't ready to. Genesis wasn't ready for it to end either. This was the best dick she ever had in the twenty-three years she had been on earth.

He pulled out, lifted her off the sink, and placed her on the ground. He racked his hands into her curly hair and gripped her head roughly. Prime gazed into her eyes. She was everything he wanted. He covered her mouth with his. Prime's lips were pressed tightly against hers. Their noses kissed, blocking her air wave, disabling her breathing. He pulled back.

"Turn around." His tone brooked no argument.

Slowly, she did as she was instructed. He lifted her effortlessly off of her feet and placed her on the same sink, this time, backwards. Her ass slightly hung off the sink. She held onto the knobs for leverage.

"Come back a little further."

She did. Her entire ass was off the sink. She used her thighs to grip the sides of the granite sink. She resembled a barrel racer with her ass a few inches in the air. Prime eased up behind her. He placed one hand around her as he used his fingers to graze her clit. He strongly gripped her pussy, and his middle finger covered her button as he slowly applied pressure, rotating it in very small circles. A soft, sexy whimper fell from her lips as her eyes rolled to the back of her head. His other hand roughly squeezed and spread her ass cheeks. He slightly dipped, came up, and thrust himself inside of her. She moaned. He grunted. He slid in and out of her wet cave. He applied more pressure to her button.

"Aaaggh! Prime!" she yelled. She placed both palms on the wall in front of her. "I'm cummin'." She felt weaker than a woman who had just given birth.

Whack! Whack! Whack!

The smacking noises echoed throughout the restroom with every thrust. He leaned in, closing up the little space between them, then stroked her kitty short and fast. Her constant moans resembled a broken record.

"I, I can't ho-hold it anymore!" she yelped as the veins in her neck protruded.

Soon she would find out that Prime could no longer hold it neither. He tried pumping his way through, hoping he wouldn't release just yet, but once his knees buckled, he knew it was pointless. A blast of euphoria exploded throughout his body as he gave his final thrust. His mind was telling him to pull out, but he just couldn't hold back.

He collapsed onto her back as he tired his damndest to control his breathing. She peered at him over her shoulder, gently placing a hand over his face, which was buried in her neck. She puckered up and he barely leaned in and kissed her lips. She pulled away and gazed into his eyes. She flashed a smile.

"I'm going back to the D with you."

He chuckled. He didn't know if she was joking or being serious. "That's cool," he replied. He grunted as he pulled out. Prime slapped her on the ass and helped her off the sink.

"Come on. We have to get out of here. No telling how long we've held these people's restroom hostage."

***

Parlay sat across from Natasha inside of her office. She had accomplished so much in the years they were separated, and he was truly proud of her. They joked about old times, laughing until they were teary-eyed. Every now and then, the images of her and her husband would flood his mental, but he couldn't bring himself to ask. That was way out of line. He couldn't defy his marriage because he doubted his wife's loyalty.

Natasha looked at Parlay before staring into space at nothing in particular. "Lay, you remember that time you got into a fight and your nose was bloody and you didn't want to go home like that, so you came to my house and I snuck you in through the window?"

Parlay chuckled, but when Natasha didn't join, he stopped. Her gaze was fixed on something outside of the massive window, but then again maybe it was nothing at all. Parlay got up and took a look for himself. He was right; there was nothing entertaining occurring outside of her window. She was in deep reverie.

He cleared his throat. "I remember," he replied, and a gang of compassion laced his words. She turned to face him.

"We——"

Knock! Knock! Knock!

An urgent knock ceased her speech and unbeknownst to Parlay, her heart as well.

"Come in," Natasha announced, frantically uncrossing her arms.

One of her employees rushed inside. Parlay had never seen the chick before, but she looked like she had just seen a ghost. He jumped into survival mode gripping the handle on the burner just to ensure it was still tucked. He had seen those eyes plenty of times before some shit popped off.

"Ms. Natasha, um, I'm sorry to interrupt." She looked from Parlay to Natasha. "Mr. Simpson is here."

Natasha gasped. She peered around as if she was looking for an exit.

Parlay's brows dipped in confusion. "What's up, Tasha? Who is Mr. Simpson? Calm down, ma." Parlay grabbed Natasha by the shoulders, forcing her to be still. Tears filled her eyes and her lips trembled as she peered at the door in fear. Parlay grabbed her jittery hands, his bafflement evident.

"Calm down, girl, I got you. Talk to me," Parlay said in a desperate tone. He really wanted to tell her there was nothing to be afraid of and that he'd protect her, but her didn't want to overstep any boundaries.

Finally, she locked eyes with Parlay. "That's my husband - well, my——"

"He's coming, Ms. Natasha!"

"You have to go, Parlay." She paused, tears brimming in her eyes.

Parlay gritted his teeth. There was no reason for a woman to be that afraid. He wanted badly to dig deeper, but his queen was at home waiting for him. He had to let the past remain in the past, because trying to position it into his present life would only destroy his future.

The look in his eyes conveyed so much concern and compassion. Natasha wanted to rebel and face the consequences later, but knowing that an early grave was a huge possibility, she quickly reconsidered.

Parlay had to make himself leave. He moved like he was battling with a forceful gust of wind and as quick as he wanted to move, he simply couldn't. He was like a paralyzed man trying to relearn to walk.

Left, right, left, right, left, right.

After all the coaxing and mental motivation, he snapped back into reality and realized he was only a few steps away from her. It was the rough tug on his arm that finally made him snap. The chick basically dragged him out of the office. He peered over his shoulder the whole time, locking eyes with a frightened Natasha.

The look of disappointment paired with uncertainty adorned his handsome face. There was a time when she and Parlay shared any and every secret, a time when they were both, best friends and lovers. Unfortunately, those times had changed and some things were better left unsaid. Her fear of her husband simply outweighed her love and concern for Parlay.

The chick led Parlay out of the office and down the lengthy hallway. Although he never saw dude, he immediately recognized him as they bypassed one another. Both men locked eyes, exchanging death glares. He was average height, but his aura was so massive it loomed, spreading throughout the hallway like a gust of wind slapping them both in the face, demanding their attention.

Parlay never broke his stare. The men exchanged threatening glares, both of them refusing to look away. Parlay stopped once he made it to the end of the hallway. His eyes fixed on the guy he'd made his opponent. Even though he told himself he wouldn't indulge in the drama, before his thoughts could even connect with his actions, he acted impulsively. He stood there motionless, eyeing the man that instilled fear in everyone else. His stance and his eyes were daring. He was looking for any sign indicating smoke. He could feel the chick tugging on his arm, but he had something to prove. He could feel her, but couldn't hear her, and truthfully, he didn't care to.

Mr. Simpson smirked and shot Parlay a wink before stepping inside of his wife's office. The small gesture infuriated him, but he simply turned and walked away.

Chapter 11
He Controls My Anxiety

Jessica felt the vibration inside of her purse. She looked around the room to assure no one was looking. Oddly, she found herself checking for Jah. She would have never admitted it to anyone other than herself. She discreetly dug her hand into her bag and grabbed her cell phone out. She hid it behind her black, leather Prada bag. It was Parlay, informing her of his arrival.

I miss your face and I can't wait to see you. A huge grin appeared across her face. Without responding, she slid her phone back inside of her purse.

The doors opened, both of them, like a scene out of a movie. It was Jah. She entered as quietly as possible in spite of the grand entrance. Her head was low and her hands were stuffed into the front of her black hoodie. She tried masking the way she felt, but it was useless. Every time she closed her eyes, she saw that text. Vivid images of Monique dressed in that teddy emerged as well. The idea of the woman she invested so much time and energy in sharing a piece of herself with someone else broke Jah into a million pieces. She hated her.

She quickly grabbed a chair and moved to the corner, the same spot she was seated in last group. She could feel eyes burning holes through the thick material, exposing every emotion that weighed deeply on her heart. There was only one person in the room that could make her feel so transparent. She pulled her hood backwards and slowly lifted her head.

Jessica dropped her head instantly, eluding Jah's candid stare. She also didn't want Jah to catch her staring, but she could hardly stop. There was something about the masculine woman that was so immersing. Thoughts loomed in her mind, but she had no plans on giving life to them. She would never risk losing her King to a female that suffered with an identity crisis.

It was Jessica's turn. "Hi, I'm Jessica, and I'm…" She paused. "I'm an addict." Quoting that line was as humiliating as getting naked in front of a group of strangers.

For the first time that day, Jah smiled.

"Thanks, Jessica. Ladies and gentlemen, today's topic will be about grief."

Jessica rolled her eyes at the mentioning of the subject. Grief had lodged into her life as a young girl and as hard as she tried ridding herself of it, nothing she did worked. It took her tears to realize that she'd be better off sheathing it until time came for her to dislodge it.

"You don't have to go into details, but in a timely manner, explain how grief has affected your life and incited your drug use."

The thought of sharing made her nervous. Unintentionally, she peered into Jah's direction and on cue, Jah did as well, forcing them to lock eyes. Jah nodded, confirming whatever she was thinking. Her pleading eyes were hoping for assurances, and she got it.

Jessica sighed deeply. She wasn't receptive to the group at all. However, she remembered how Jah explained the significance of participating during group. *After this group, you'll have six left,* she coaxed herself. She stared down at her fidgety fingers, thinking of what she would say. She was hoping group would end before they made it around the entire circle.

It was Jah's turn. She stood to her feet. Unbeknownst, to everyone else Jah had stage freight. She had always been told to look at someone or something you find comfort in. As much as she wanted to fix her gaze on the beauty a few feet away from her, she fixed them on the wall behind Jessica, where a Malcolm X portrait adorned the wall. She cleared her throat.

For the first time in a long time, Jessica could clearly see those eyes. They were as mesmerizing as the first day she peered into them. However, they had definitely changed. That desperation was so visible that she instantly sympathized with her. Naturally, grief had that affect.

"Grief affected me because every time I lose someone especially close to my heart…" Her words became choppy as she swallowed the huge lump in her throat. "I'll use drugs to numb the pain." She paused. She opened her mouth, but nothing came out. She peered up at the ceiling as she rocked on the balls of her feet. Everyone sat attentively waiting in anticipation for anything to fall from her lips, even Jessica. She loosened and tightened her mouth. Anyone with eyes could see the despair. Something weighed heavy on her heart, and she yearned to release whatever it was they clung to her like a web, but she couldn't. She needed help; she needed someone other than herself, strength that she didn't have at the moment because her issues had drained her. Finally, she sat down. However, everyone continued to stare at her, hoping she'd say something then.

Jessica clapped loudly, indicating that Jah was done sharing so that everyone could direct their attention someplace else. They joined in as well, then passed the invisible mic to the next member. Seldomly, Jah and Jessica would lock eyes., neither of them wanting the other to know they were looking in the first place, so they'd lower their heads or look away quickly.

The clock read 6:50 p.m. It was ten minutes until class ended, and there were three people in front of Jessica. If she could just wait for ten more minutes, she could make it through the group without touching on such a sensitive subject. Involuntarily, she wondered if hers and Jah's pain stemmed from the same place. *What loved ones had she lost? What pain did she and does she numb?* She wouldn't dare ask such questions loud enough to be heard. However, she did think it.

She was so caught up in her thoughts she didn't hear Bella call her name. She actually called it several times before Jessica acknowledged her.

"Yes, yes, I'm sorry," she blurted shamefully. Realizing that she had not dodged the uncomfortable topic, she sighed deeply. She wanted badly to just birth every negative thought, leave, and never come back. However, doing so would result in prison time. She lifted her bag from her lap, stood to her feet, and placed the bag on the chair. Those same group of people she sneered at were the same ones that snipped her confidence. She hasn't realized she was so perturbed until now.

Breathe, Jessica.

She sighed deeply and placed her hands on her hips. She peered around the room and found comfort at a spot on the wall. It appeared chipped, as if someone had peeled the paint off, but it was definitely defective. She found comfort in the odd shape because she could relate to how it must've felt being the only flaw in the room. Present but unnoticed because all of her dirty laundry was up to her neck, covering up the person she truly was. She wished she could've found comfort in Jah like Jah found comfort in her.

"Hi, my name is Jessica, and grief is what completely changed my life." She paused. Jessica tilted back her head to prevent the tears from falling. "On October 6, 2010, I watched my mother take her own life. It didn't broach drugs or alcohol, but it did broach other addictive behaviors."

Her revelation tugged at Jah's heartstrings, mainly because of her burning desire to rush to her side and console her. She wanted to kiss the tears as they fell, but instead, she had to watch Jessica roughly wipe them away on her own, just like she had to deal with it in her own. Or did she? Jah wondered, of course, if she had someone. The beautiful ones were always taken or they were in a forced entanglement due to their ex-lover's territorial mentality or abusive obsession.

"That's group! Yay, group!" Bella yelled.

Everybody stood and recited the serenity prayer. Jessica had her bag on her shoulder and was standing by the door, waiting eagerly to leave. She just wanted to climb into bed and bury herself under her husband's arms.

Reliving that moment always left Jessica feeling snubbed, because she was way too young to lose her mother and her mother was too young to have lost her life in spite of the situation. She felt inadequate because she wasn't capable of stopping her from causing harm, or good enough for her mother to fight through her plights so that she could be a part of her life. She dashed through the lot to her car.

Jah wasn't too far behind. She was ready to go home and unwind as well. Monica had been calling and texting her nonstop, but she refused to respond. Little did Monique know, her fate was sealed the day Jah found those messages. There was simply no coming back from that. Time wouldn't even heal those wounds and if it did, Jah would be too old to wipe her own ass, let alone fret if someone was lying next to her. She stopped in her tracks as she took the pitiful sight in. She slowly made her way to the other side of her Challenger to see if those tires were on flat as well. Sadly, they were.

"Fuck!" she yelled in frustration. She harshly slammed her hand against the trunk. She knew it wasn't anyone but Monique's ass. She bit down so hard on her lip she was sure she had drawn blood. "Aarrgghh!" She clenched her fist, tightening every muscle in her body. She wanted to break the bone that held her eye intact she was so irked.

Jessica peered out of her window in fear, looking around swiftly to see what the noise had come from.

Jah was so annoyed she was on the brink of tears. She unclench her fist and tilted her head towards the sky. *Breathe, Jah, just breathe.*

She placed her hands on top of her head and panted. After taking a few deep breaths and calming herself down, she peered around in search of a solution. *I just got to holler at Joey.* It was that simple. Joey was a friend of hers down the street that owed a tire shop. It would cost her some money she didn't want to spend, but she had no other choice. She patted her pockets on her sweats for her phone. Suddenly, she remembered that she had left her phone at the house on the charger.

Fuck!

She peered around the lot. Her eyes immediately landed on Jessica's. She lowered her head and pinched the bridge of her nose. She sighed, mentally prepping herself to approach her. Her full lips appeared and disappeared as she headed towards Jessica. Jessica's door was still ajar, leaving the lights in her car on. She walked up on her side of the car from behind. She ran her fingers through her curly hair and roughly ran them down her face.

"Aye," Jah spoke in a whispered tone. She placed her hand on the corner of her door, opening it a little.

Jessica jolted in fear. She placed her hand over her heart and panted once realizing it was Jah. "You scared the shit out of me," she voiced one she silenced her pounding heart. A look of confusion etched Jessica's face. "What's up?" she asked, peering up at Jah. She could tell Jah was bothered.

"I need a favor. I can pay you," she offered.

"What is it?" Because money isn't an issue," she shot back.

Arrogant ass. Jah peered over her shoulder and rolled her eyes so that Jessica couldn't see her. "Somebody flattened my tires and I just need a ride to the tire shop down the street," Jah reluctantly admitted. She shook her head before the words fell from her mouth.

"Nah, I don't trust people in my car. Motherfuckas crazy these days," she responded, pretending to be unconcerned with Jah and her issues. Inwardly, she did care. She was even curious to know who flattened her tires and why because it was an uncommon act.

Jah stared at her in utter disbelief. She didn't understand how people could so cruel. Jah's eyes imparted so much disgust, Jessica considered apologizing. However, she had to remain stiff for her own purposes.

Unbeknownst to Jah, Jessica shamefully found herself being slightly attracted to the woman who possessed many masculine features. So, to avoid acting on it, she had to assure that she stayed far away from it. She kept trying to mentally convince herself that intimacy with a woman was whimsical and disgusting, yet her body felt the total opposite. The flutter in her chest when she would see Jah. The urge to look for her whenever she wasn't around and the way her pussy throbbed whenever Jah would give her that penetrating gaze or Jessica would catch her licking her full, juicy, heart-shaped lips. Diamond had mentioned several times how satisfying oral sex was with a woman. She would be lying if she said she never envisioned Jah being between her legs.

Jah turned and walked away. "Cool," she voiced, striding to her vehicle.

Jessica's leg shook uncontrollably as she fought with the voice in her head. She didn't think Jah would be so defeated, although, she had every right to be.

Stop her!

She wanted to take off in the direction she was walking in.

JUST GO!

Jessica slammed her door shut and turned the volume on her music all the way up to drown out that pestering voice in her head. She gripped and slowly twisted the steering wheel as she rocked back and forth.

Fuck it.

She sped off before she gave in, allowing her conscience to make her change her mind. She figured if she could just make it home and crawl under the man she wanted desperately to make love to, she wouldn't feel remorseful about what she had done to Jah.

A smile spread across her face as soon as she opened the door to her home and Chris Brown lyrics spilled out. Hope filled her eyes as she moved at a quicker pace to get to her man. Lit candles were positioned sporadically throughout the house. She didn't know what the occasion was. She just hoped this was his way of telling her that he stopped taking his medicine for a few days and was ready to take her down. Parlay's dick was addictive, especially since it was the best she ever had. However, with him not being able to get and keep an erection, Jessica felt deprive, like an imprisoned woman. Women in prison had better chances of getting a hard dick than she did because if they tried hard enough, they could just fuck an officer. Jessica, however, had tried everything there was to try. The only thing left was to invite another woman into the bed in hopes the two of them could arouse him enough, but her pride and self-respect wouldn't allow her to do such thing.

Her smile abruptly faded, her heart stopped beating, and her juices quit flowing as she gasped sharply. Parlay was lying across the bed sound asleep. Jessica pouted and smacked her lips.

She dragged to the bed, dropping her purse and keys on the night stand. Tears fell as she began to undress, one piece at a time. She pretended that he was awake, demanding she strip down to her birthday suit. Bare as the day she was pushed from her mother's womb, Jessica climbed into bed with her husband. The inside of her thighs were already wet from the anticipation just from the front door to her bedroom. She slowly climbed on top of his bare chest as he lay on his back clad in nothing but his Ethika briefs. Afraid that he would awake and see her tears, she reached over and grabbed her head wrap off of the bed rail and covered his eyes. Jessica caressed his strong, muscular chest with her small soft hands. Unable to resist the urge, she leaned down and planted soft, wet pecks all over him. She reached her arms underneath him and clung to him like someone would if they were doing pull-ups on a steel bar. She held him tightly as more tears fell. The wetness dripped on his chest and rolled into the crease of his neck, causing Parlay to stir. He opened his eyes, but everything was black. He wrapped his arms around the weight on his chest.

She was curvy and soft as his hands traveled from her ribs down her spine to her ass then her thighs. He dipped his hands towards the wetness that soaked his stomach. He coated his fingers and brought it to his nose. He softly groaned in excitement, slightly lifting his ass off the bed. The small gesture sent Jessica's hormones into a frenzy. She slightly leaned up and passionately pressed her lips against his. He placed both hands in the center if he plump ass cheeks and firmly gripped, them spreading them apart. He stuck his tongue between her top and bottom lip, invading her mouth. She gladly invited him in. Slowly, their tongues danced as moans and grunts filled the room.

Parlay slightly scooted her forward with his forearm as he swiftly pushed down his briefs with his other hand, releasing the beast out of his cage. He relaxed the grip he had on Jessica's back. As soon as she felt his stuff pole against her ass cheek, she gasped in shock. She lifted up abruptly and reached behind her to see if it was real or if she was imagining things. Parlay's pole was pointed towards the ceiling, stiff as concrete. She swiftly hopped off his chest and covered her mouth in awe. She was elated and appalled to see his meaty nine inches standing at attention. A thick vein ran from the base up to his perfect mushroom tip.

Jessica's mouth watered. Like a magnetic force, she crawled to it and wrapped her hands around it. He gazed unblinking and rooted. Parlay eased his hands to his head and secured the head wrap over his eyes. The feel of the unknown was odd, but intriguing. He sat up, and Jessica released her grip and scooted back.

Parlay eased off the bed. He pulled the briefs all the way down to his ankles and stepped out of them, one leg at a time. He inched closer to the bed and felt around on top of the sheets. He patted around until he felt her. He rubbed up and down her legs until he came in contact with her knees. He reached underneath them and pulled her closer until she was at the edge. He stuck his entire hand over and against her box, instantly lubricating it. Parlay wrapped that same hand around his dick and lightly stroked it. Jessica's kitty throbbed in anticipation. Slowly, he fell to his knees. Jessica placed her feet on his shoulders Parlay pressed his nose against, under, and around her opening.

He grunted, pleased with her tantalizing scent. He planted kisses on her plump lips and instantly she reached. Her back arched and her mouth fell open as Parlay pulled the top back to uncover her pearl. He attacked it slowly, passionately, applying major pressure ,then taking it away.

"I missed you," he whispered between kisses. "Tell me you missed me too."

"I-I missed you," she moaned as he brought her to an orgasm.

She felt so good and tasted so great on his tongue that even after she came, he kept going, arousing her all over again. She busted three times before she couldn't take anymore. She wanted Parlay inside of her.

"Parlay, please fuck me," she begged between breaths as her chest rose and fell.

Parlay stood to his feet he pulled Jessica closer. Her body slightly hung off the edge. Flesh to flesh, he grabbed his penis and rubbed it against her wet center. Moans and grunts filled the room. The anticipation alone was about to make Parlay bust. He rubbed the tip of his dick against her pearl, down her opening, and further down the crack of her ass. Jessica lay there with her shaky legs wrapped tightly around him.

"Parlay!" she hollered in frustration. She was ready to see what that dick do.

Swiftly and without warning, he plunged deep inside her. "Ugggh!" she yelped in pain, but pain had never felt so good. He pulled out and did it again.

She dug her nails into his sweaty back as he grabbed her plump ass firmly and began rocking and rolling inside of her warm, wet tightness. He lifted one of her legs, pushing it backwards, then slowly dug in her tunnel at an angle. He was chipping off pieces of her soul with every stroke. Tears fell and filled inside of her ears as she lay there enjoying every second.

"Ooohh, Lay, I-I love you," she moaned. She eased her finger down to her box and pressed her finger against her clit and applied pressure. Her body jerked wildly. It had been months since she felt so much pleasure.

He pinned both legs back and fed her short, quick strokes. Her eyes rolled back and everything went limp.

With the touch of energy she did have, she moved her hand in a circular motion around her button. She couldn't tell which orgasm would come first. He roughly spread her ass cheeks further apart, causing her flower to open wider. He slammed all nine inches inside of her ruthlessly, forcing Jessica to cry out in pleasure and pain. Effortlessly, he flipped her over, her finger never ceasing.

"Toot that ass up," he said as he slapped her ass, stinging her.

Jessica sank her chest all the way to the bed, which caused her behind to stick up higher and her tunnel to open wider. However, Parlay wanted some of that, so he dug in between her thighs, ridding her of her juices. He used it as a lubricant, rubbing the sticky liquid around her opening. He moved his hands from her shoulder down her back and firmly placed his hands on her ass. Taking a deep breath, he tapped at her back door before thrusting inside an inch at a time.

"Ssssss," she hissed. Her finger stopped. The pain was immeasurable. "Fuck!" Jessica shouted.

"You a big girl. Take that dick," he voiced, swatting her hand down, which she had placed on his thigh to prevent him from going any further.

Swiftly, she turned and buried her head into the sheet. There was a loud but muffled sound as Parlay thrust the last few inches inside of her. He moved inside of her gently and slowly. The pain was starting to transform into pleasure, so Jessica used her finger to resume its attack. Her clit was swollen and throbbing. She was on the brink of an orgasm - two, to be exact. Her muscles loosened up, giving him a touch more access to stroke her how wanted to. He moved his hands to her waist and stroked her long, hard, and deep. She threw it back at him, matching him stroke for stroke. Parlay's legs buckled.

"Oh my God!" she moaned as she came to an orgasm. Her arm went limp as a noodle.

"Hell yeah, throw that shit," Parlay cheered her on. He gritted his teeth as he felt the nut beginning to rise. "Shit," he mumbled. He pushed Jessica down, forcing her flat on her stomach. He placed one arm underneath her stomach and the other around her throat. He dug inside of her with his chest pressed against her back. He held her tightly, as if she would magically slip away. He quickened his pace, then slowed. He dug around a little bit, and then sped up again. "I love you," he whispered into her ear between breaths.

"I love you too," she whispered. If he wasn't so close, he wouldn't have heard her, it was so faint. "I've always loved you and will always love you."

A loud roar fell from his lips as he released everything in him, inside of her.

Chapter 12
Say Something

"It's good to hear you in a good mood. You all giddy and shit," Diamond spoke into the receiver.

"I don't mean to brag, but bae put in work last night," Jessica bragged as she quickly moved around the house, preparing for her class.

Diamond could hear the excitement in her voice. She smiled in satisfaction. Jessica had become uptight and a bit negative since her sex life crashed and burned. Finally, she had her friend back. "Girl, I'm so happy for you. So, um…" Diamond paused. "Is the problem fixed, or…you know."

"Well, I wouldn't say it's completely fixed, but he stopped taking his medication for few days, so he's good for now."

"Okay." Diamond scowled. Immediately, she wondered why Parlay hadn't let up on his medication a long time ago.

Jessica chuckled. "Bitch, I was just about to commit a sin, but li'l Lay came through."

Diamond joined the laughter. "Girl, you wasn't about to do shit."

They chatted aimlessly for a little while longer. Jessica talked up until she pulled into that lot where her class was located. She wanted to fish around a bit to see if Jah was still upset with her for not giving her a ride, so she made sure she arrived ten minutes early. For the first time since attending the class, she was eager to go inside.

The cloud that once dampened her spirit didn't do so today. Instead of dragging, she strutted up to the double doors and made her way inside. Everyone was prepping for class. The usual menu was positioned in the center of the table: three dozen glazed donuts, a box of sweeteners, and two containers of fresh vanilla creamer to enhance the Maxwell coffee brewing in the coffee machine.

Jessica's eyes moved twice as fast as her legs. She gripped her clutch tightly with two hands as she strutted towards the table. Discreetly, she scanned the crowd around the table. Jah wasn't in it. Usually she'd skip refreshments, but not tonight. She used the machine for good positioning, enabling her to peer around the room without looking obvious. Her heart raced in anticipation in hopes she'd see her, but she didn't. Slowly, she made a cup of coffee and grabbed a doughnut out of the box. She learned against the table, nibbling on the doughnut and sipping on the coffee. She cut her eyes in the direction of the door every time she heard it open, but it wasn't Jah.

"Two minutes til group, ladies!" Bells announced.

Jessica rolled her eyes in irritation, dejection stealing her elation. Jessica would never admit it but, she was upset. Slowly, she wiped her hands, trashed the cup, and moved towards her chair. As soon as her ass hit the suede, the door opened and this time it was Jah. Hopefully, Jessica peered back at Jah with a tight-lipped smile, but Jah looked past her instead.

"You have a minute to grab refreshments," Bella told Jah from across the room.

Jessica wanted to dash to the table, but the humiliation would've been costly.

"Eric, do you mind if Jah sits right here?" Jessica asked the guy on the side of her.

Eric shrugged and stood to his feet. He sat across the room in a different chair. Jah slowly made her towards the group, slowly eyeing and stirring the coffee in the Dixie cup. She almost by-passed the seat Jessica had saved for her when she heard her name being called. As hard as it was for Jessica to do such brave act, she did it.

The room was quiet, all eyes on them. Jah turned around and eyed Jessica grimly. Her gazed imparted so much repugnance. Jessica hesitated. Jah widened her eyes, indicating for her to spit it out.

"Um, I'm sorry, I just wanted to tell you, I, uh, saved you a seat."

Jah scowled. "Bruh, I don't want to sit by you." She headed towards her corner and sat alone like she had done many times before.

Jessica felt degraded as a mother who just lost her kids to CPS. She had never felt such amount of humiliation. She ignored the stares that she could feel looming around the circle. She wanted to run out of the building and into her car, but instead, she gripped her clutch and tried forgetting what just occurred.

Oddly, after everything that happened, Jessica found herself peering towards the corner in the spot she sat. However, Jah wasn't even engaged in group. Her head was low, eyes to the floor as she fidgeted with her fingers. Jessica wondered what was going on with her inwardly.

"Yay, group!"

All of them immediately prayed the serenity prayer aloud immediately after. However, Jah didn't. When Jessica lifted her head and opened her eyes, Jah was gone. She rushed out of the building as well. A loud dispute slowed her steps. She peered around frantically to see where it was coming from and suddenly Jah appeared in her view. She wasn't alone. She stood there bickering with a female. Jessica walked closer to get a better look and hear what was being said. It was as if the chick was trying to get Jah to stop and listen or at least slow down.

"Bruh, move, get out the way. We done, Mo," Jah voiced angrily, pushing her backwards.

"No, I want you to listen to me, Jah I miss you. I'm sorry. She can't love me, touch me, fuck me, care for me like you. Please!" she begged.

"You can save them tears for a bitch that cares about them 'cause I don't. You sealed your fate when you made plans with that bitch." Jah stepped forward; Mo stepped backwards. Finally, they reached Jah's car. Her jaw dropped in bewilderment. "Bitch, you flattened my tires again?" She firmly gripped and tugged on the hair atop of her head.

Jah mushed Monique in the head harshly, causing her to swiftly stumble backwards and land on her ass. She rushed her and lifted her foot. Monique's arms covered her face as she braced herself for the beating.

"Jah, wait!" Jessica rushed over and stood in front of Jah. "You kick her ass, you going to jail. It's not worth it, come on."

Jah smacked her lips and waved Jessica off. She didn't want to admit it, but Jessica was right. Her heart was pounding in her chest and her adrenaline was at an all-time high. She just wanted to destroy something, someone, anything. Jah let out a long, low sound, indicating her pain. She wanted to scream, cry, and curse, but she didn't.

Jessica caressed her arm. "Come on. I'll take you to the tire shop."

Jah peered down at her, a bit reluctant, but she turned and walked away anyways, leaving Monique bawling on the concrete. Jah followed behind Jessica panting with clenched fists. She didn't calm down until minutes later. The Meek Mill *Expensive Pain* album had calmed her spirit. She was so repulsed she didn't even notice the car hadn't moved.

"My bad," Jah said, scratching her head as she tapped her screen, activating her GPS. She set her iPhone inside of the cup holder. The operator chimed in and Jessica drove off the lot.

The tire shop was only twelve minutes away, making her feel quite unnerved. Whatever she had to say she only had a short amount of time to do so. Perhaps she didn't have anything to say at all. The music was loud enough to be heard, but low enough for them to hear each other as well. However, Jessica could hear herself breathing. She wondered if Jah could hear it too.

Please say something.

She slowed, then stopped at the red light. The silence made her a bit uncomfortable, so she reached into her console and applied some of her Victoria's Secret lip gloss. Jah cleared her throat. Jessica's heart stopped in hunger. Her hopes immediately died once she figured out that was it. Just a fucking cough.

They pulled up at the tire shop. It was very dark.

"I'll be right back," Jah said, hopping out of her car.

Jessica checked her phone and sent a quick text to Parlay. *Getting something to eat, I'll be there in a few.* She peered through the mirror on her phone, puckering up her soft full lips.

A soft knock at her window forced her to jolt in her fear. "Shit! You scared me." She sighed deeply, clutching her heart. She let the window down.

"My bad," Jah apologized. "Let me get this." Jah leaned inside of her car. Her Kenneth Cole cologne infiltrated Jessica's nostrils, immediately making her pussy pulsate. The heat of Jah's body radiated off her, sending chills down Jessica's spine. She closed her legs in hopes of ceasing the pleasurable annoyance in between her legs.

Jah reached over Jessica to grab her phone. She could feel and smell the sweet scent coming from Jessica's nostrils, she was so close. Jah grabbed her phone then she accidentally dropped it on the floor of the passenger's side.

"I got it," Jessica obliged. She leaned over and effortlessly picked up the phone. She raised back up, her lips almost colliding with Jah's. Her heart raced vigorously. Their eyes locked. Jah conveyed her lust paired with fear. Jessica conveyed her lust paired with confidence.

I got you if you just let me. You don't have to be scared, Jah thought, holding her gaze.

It was as if everything stopped and silenced. You could no longer hear cars bypassing, chatter from the men posted up in front of the gas station across the street, or anything else that would distract them from the moment they both secretly desired.

Jah leaned in and covered Jessica's mouth with hers. They shared passionate, soft slow pecks while peering into each other's eyes. Jessica felt like Jah was looking into her soul, trying to decipher if it was love or just. Jah placed a hand behind her neck, pulling Jessica closer. She wanted to slide her tongue down her throat, but she didn't want to overwhelm her. She had dealt with many straight women in her past. Slow was the best way to move with them. Instead, she brushed her lips against hers. Jah found her bottom lip, placed it between her lips, then gently and passionately sucked it. Jah used her thumb to stroke the slide of Jessica's face. She released her lips, pressed her lips against hers, and placed another one in the center of her forehead.

"Thanks," Jah said, slowly backpedaling away from the window, leaving Jessica stunned and perplexed.

Chapter 13
Your Side of the Bed

Lately, shit had weighed so heavy on Parlay's heart that he thought it would burst from the amount of pressure. He had let Prime take a few days off, considering the hard work he had been putting in. Prime wasted no time. He left for Atlanta that same night. Out of everyone in his life, Prime had knowledge of most of Parlay's issues. Although it was more than what everyone else knew, it was mediocre compared to the entire truth.

Parlay popped three Xanax and headed downtown to Dr. Haskins's suite. He needed to calm the anxiety. Since meeting with her, he had kept it very dry and short, unsure if she was honest enough to be trusted. Parlay's past had left him with so many wounds. Many of them had healed, turning into scars. However, his ability to trust was his deepest wound and it appeared fresh as the day it was inflicted. But today, he was going to let his guard down. It was time that he allowed Dr. Haskins further into his life, and maybe she could give him the feedback he needed. However, no feedback would be fine as well. Really all he needed was to voice some of the shit he kept hidden inside for so long.

***

Back at the house, Jessica moved around swiftly with her phone pressed against her ear. She had been trying to call Diamond since Parlay left the house this morning. She still wasn't picking up the phone. Guilt had her running around her two-story home, decorating the house and preparing a meal in honor of Parlay. She found it quite strange how her body reacted to Jah. In spite of the amazing, baby-making sex she and Parlay had two nights prior, she still yearned for something different. Perhaps it was because she wasn't sure when she would get it again since their sex life solely depended on when and if Parlay took his medicine.

A variety of seasonings decorated the counters around the sink area. She ran around the spacious kitchen, frustrated and panicky. Jessica was a great cook. Today, she felt obligated because of her disloyal acts, which she had never even considered communicating until she met Jah.

Bing!

Her phone chirped. It was either a notification from her Facebook, Instagram ,or her email account. She dashed towards the living room and grabbed her phone off the coffee table. It was Facebook. Since Facebook was the least of her concerns at the moment, she simply looked at the screen in annoyance. She was about to place her phone inside of her makeshift apron when the name on the profile stole her attention and her breath. She gasped sharply. It was Jah.

Jessica found it ironic that at the instant she had been thinking of Jah, evidently Jah was thinking about her too. Afraid to simply accept the request and her request alone, she decided to add the three other users who had sent her friend requests days ago. She had intentionally shunned the three women request cognizant of their intentions. All three of them had some sort of intentions. All three of them had some sort of association with Parlay in the past. Obviously, they were all concerned with his future as well. Jessica held her breath as she accepted all four friend requests. Immediately, her phone sounded again.

Bing!

A new message had shown up in her inbox. Jessica's eyes were fastened on the screen as she quickly tapped the notification on the screen. She blinked rapidly seeing that the message was from Jah. Her head swiveled around in fear. She appeared timid as a child who was trying to commit a sinful act while their parents were home. Although Parlay wasn't even home, instinctively she was on heightened alert. She tapped the screen, opening the message.

Jah: can we talk?

Jessica scowled at the message like it had been typed backwards. She simply didn't know how to respond.

Bing!

Jah: can we talk now?

Jessica heart banged so loudly in her chest that it rattled her insides.

Jessica: What's up? Talk, I'm listening.

She peered over her shoulder at the shrimp and sausages she had boiling in the pot, but her feet were glued to the carpet. She waited in anticipation. The food was now her least concern. She peered down at the lavender AP, but it was pointless since she didn't know when Parlay would be returning.

Jessica: I miss your face. What time you coming home?

Bing!

It was another message from Jah.

Jah: I don't need you to just listen. I need you to feel me. Can we meet up, or can I slide through? I just need ten minutes.

Startled, Jessica's eyes widened. She nibbled on the inside of her cheek as she gawked at the screen in disbelief. Jah was definitely bold. Too bold, actually. Yet it definitely whetted her interest. This time when her phone chimed, it was Parlay.

Parlay: Give me at least another hour. I have to link up with Prime.

Prime wasn't due to return until tomorrow, but Jessica didn't know that and there was no way he could admit his therapy sessions.

Bing!

Jah: Drop your location.

Damn, she's adamant.

Her heart fluttered in anticipation paired with concern. However, the thrill of it all predominated her fears of being caught. She darted to the kitchen, turned the food on low, and sent Jah the instructions she had requested. Her impetuous movements were sloppy, but she didn't slow her stride. She wiped her counters down and placed all the contents on one side, making it look as neat as possible.

Ding! Ding!

The sound of the doorbell made Jessica immobilized. The only thing moving was her mouth as she mouthed obscenities to no one in particular. Finally, she patted her bundles down and scanned the living room area for anything out of place before opening the door. She placed her hand on the knob, lifted her other hand to her mouth, and blew her breath into it, cupping it over both her nose and mouth.

Okay I'm good.

She yanked the immense wooden door open, instantly, scowling in confusion. "Diamond?" she asked.

Diamond wasted no time stepping inside. "You act like you surprised to see me," Diamond commented, setting her bag on the couch, making herself at home.

Slowly, Jessica closed the door, her mouth agape. Evidently, she was still in shock. "Actually…" Jessica paused, forcing a tight-lipped smile. Although what she was about to reveal was against any and everything she allegedly stood for, she would rather Diamond glorify in her chagrin than anyone else. "I'm glad you showed up unannounced because I really need a favor," Jessica said her face lacking emotion. She knew the moment the unknown fell from her lips, there would be plenty laughter and "I told you so."

"What's up? You know I got you. If I handle that, can I make me a plate of whatever that is you up in hea' cooking?" she joked.

"Funny that you asked, because I'm going to need you to finish it."

Diamond's brows dipped in confusion. "That's cool, but where you going?" Diamond asked.

"I'm not going anywhere, but someone is coming over!"

A slow smile crept up on Diamonds face. "Bitch, who?"

Jessica clenched her jaws, then sighed deeply. "Jah." With her eyes on the ground, she whispered the name softy. Diamond would've heard her if she was standing directly next to her.

"Bitch, who?" she asked again, her face balled up like she had just eaten something sour.

Jessica swallowed the lump in her throat. "Jah," she voiced sternly, crossing her arms over her chest.

Diamond took a step back. She squinted, tapping the tip of her index finger against her chin as she plugged the name into her memory bank, hoping an image would appear. "Jah, Jah, Jah, Jah," she repeated, pacing the floor in a circle. "The name so familiar, but I don't remember this Jah dude for some reason," she admitted, her face full of concern. "Make me remember," she stated, placing her hands on her hip. She didn't give a damn. She was determined to figure it out.

She peered into Diamond's eyes. She wondered if Diamond could sense the vexation. Jessica lowered her head again, but quickly tossed it back. "You not gon' remember dude 'cause it's the chick from the strip club." Jessica reluctantly admitted.

Diamond gasped sharply. A low, slow chuckle fell from her lips. She wagged her fingers and slowly shook her head. "Wait, wait, not *miss strictly dickly*. Run that back for me one more time." Sarcasm laced her words.

Jessica smacked her lips and stormed off towards the kitchen. Diamond ran after her, instantly catching up to her. She grabbed her by the forearm and spun her around, forcing Jessica to give her undivided attention.

"No, Diamond, I don't want to talk about it, that's why I haven't told you!"

Diamond wrapped her arms around Jessica's midsection. "Aww, baby, don't be mad at me. You know I ride with you whatever you do. I wouldn't be Diamond if I didn't."

A half smile crept on Jessica face as she hugged her friend back. Diamond leaned back with a smile so massive you could see all thirty-two teeth.

"Now tell me everything. You better not leave out a single detail."

Jessica was in the middle of running Diamond all the details when the doorbell sounded. Jessica gasped sharply. "Shit, that's her!" she blurted, her eyes wide as golf balls.

"I'll finish the food," Diamond offered.

"Cool," Jessica said, then paused as she removed her apron. "Look, I need you to keep an eye out for Parlay as well, but if something happens to arise for any reason, we going to pretend that Jah is your boo."

"Bet," Diamond agreed while nodding her head quickly.

Jessica rid her clothes of any noticeable debris and darted to the living area. She looked in the peephole and unlocked the locks as her heart begin to pound in anticipation. She opened the door. Jah stood there with her hands buried inside of her pockets.

Damn, this bitch look finger lickin' good.

Jah's face fade and line up was so immaculate, it made Jessica's button buzz in avidity. Although she was adorned in expensive threads, her eyes were by far the most captivating, capturing her mind, body, and soul simultaneously.

"Look, I'll just be real quick." Jah held her hands up in surrender.

Jessica peered down at her watch. "Cool, you have about ten minutes."

Jah slyly grinned and gladly stepped inside. Diamond hovered over the stove, pretending that their presence didn't bother her. However, as soon as the two bypassed the living area and moved towards the rear of the house, she stopped stirring and sprinted out of the kitchen and into the hallway to get a closer peek. She and Jessica locked eyes in the nick of time. Jessica winked and Diamond grinned until the gaze was blocked by the wooden door which separated them.

Jah was leaning against the dresser when Jessica turned around, her arms crossed at the chest and her legs crossed at the ankles. She wondered if Jessica could sense the slight discomfort. Jah could surely sense hers. She broke eye contact, and it only made Jah stare even harder.

Jah cleared her throat. "I want you, Jessica."

Jessica moved away from the door and slowly eased to the edge of the bed. Her hand hung low as she gazed down at nothing in particular. *This chick is bold.* Jessica placed strands of her hair behind her ear as she swallowed the lump in her throat. Her masquerade of confidence had vanished as she peered up at Jah through sheepish eyes. "What do you mean, Jah? You know that I'm married," she admitted. Besides the time she had given Jah a ride to the tire shop, this was the first time she had felt so much nervous energy.

"That's fine, but I just got to have you." Jessica opened her mouth too protest, but Jah spoke up, ceasing her speech all at once. She moved away from the desk and closer to Jessica. Maybe it was because she was sitting now and Jah was so tall, but she didn't remember feeling that small in her presence earlier. Knowing her motives and ability to sternly voice them intimidated Jessica more than standing in front of her ass naked. "You know you want me too."

"If I did, we'd be fucking."

Jah watched Jessica silently, wondering why she was not reacting like most women would to this opportunity. Jah shrugged and eased her hands back into her pockets. "We'll need to set a date, 'cause obviously we can't do it here."

Jessica shook her head. *Is she hard of hearing?* "Jah, I told you, I'm married. I'm not——"

Jah bent down and leaned in, pressing her soft and lush lips against Jessica's. The kiss was of both lust and respect. Her fingers felt good in Jessica's hair as well as her tongue in her mouth. It felt good to Jah as well. Jah eased up and moves towards the door.

"I'll drop you the location," she continued. "We'll set a good date for the both of us." Jah paused with her hand on the doorknob.

Jessica opened her mouth to object again, but the only word she managed to utter was "Alright." She didn't even get off the bed to see if Jah let herself out. Hopefully she did. She was in no shape to follow behind her. She had to gather her thoughts, which seemed to have left the room with Jah. Jessica couldn't believe Jah could open, read, and comprehend her so well. She stood to her feet and immediately she could feel her juices trickling down her leg.

Shit

She rushed out of her bedroom.

Diamond was leaning against the counter. She appeared to be sampling the food. "Let me find out that young'un put you to bed?" she joked in between bites.

Jessica's left brow raised. She found Diamond's little comment quite amusing. "I'm not about to entertain you. Did you finish cooking?" Jessica asked, opening the tops on the pots. The smell was irresistible.

"Yep," Diamond answered proudly. Her response was short and dry, but her gaze was the total opposite. She wanted to know more about what transpired between the two of them.

"Okay, I'm about to hop in the shower real quick." Jessica took off without giving Diamond the opportunity to respond. She tossed her clothes inside of the bin and showered quickly before Parlay arrived. She was lotioning her body when the door to her bathroom opened. She was just in time - well, she thought she was until she met the familiar and oddly hungry eyes of her best friend. Jessica's brows dipped in confusion as her face contorted offensively. "Diamond what are you doing?" Jessica questioned.

Diamond wore a mischievous smirk on her face as she pushed the door to the bathroom open further. She tugged on the thin string that kept her robe together and it opened up like a curtain.

Unconsciously, Jessica inspected her body each asset at a time, her curiosity growing by the second. Jessica had seen Diamond's body plenty of times before but it was as if she was looking through a different set of eyes this time. Diamond inched closer.

"I just want to give you a sample of what Jah is going to give you. Besides, I've been waiting on you to cross over to the other side for a long time, Jess."

The anticipation in her voice sent chills down Jessica's spine. She had never viewed her friend in any other form but as her friend. It turned her on and embarrassed her at the same time. Diamond had never showed such signs. Perhaps, Jessica was heedless to them.

Diamond took her silence as a go. She pulled Jessica against her until their bare chests met. They both inhaled sharp breaths. The warmth of Diamond's body created a sensation that she didn't want to pull away from. What Jessica thought would be awkward was actually arousing. Diamond begin kissing her way down Jessica's neck, her breath coming in harsh ripples against her skin. "Let's go to the bed," Diamond whispered against her throat. She held her hand out. Jessica place her hand into Diamond's and she led the way.

"This shit is kind of weird, Diamond," Jessica admitted as they stopped in front of her bed. "I at least need a drink or something."

Diamond left the room to fetch her a drink immediately. Whatever Jessica needed to make herself feel comfortable, she was going to do it. A minute or so later, she returned with a short glass of Jose Cuervo, no ice and nothing to chase it with. Jessica was standing in the same spot Diamond had left her in.

She stood there timidly like the new chick at the strip club who was about to perform on stage for the first time. Jessica guzzled the drink down immediately. She was a nervous wreck. She tilted her head backwards so that she could get every drop. Diamond used her fingertip to trace Jessica's soft nipples, which hardened instantly. Jessica quivered a bit. Afraid to look down and face the awkwardness, she twirled her tongue around the glass, assuring she got every drop.

Diamond replaced her mouth with her tongue. She wrapped her arms around Jessica's back and pulled her closer. Her lips close softly over her nipple, and Jessica's eyes shut involuntary. Chills erupted over her skin as Diamond's hands began to explore every bare part of her back and down to her soft, plump ass. She lightly squeezed both cheeks. The buzz from the alcohol slowly faded in like a beat. Diamond reached up and took the cup out of Jessica's hand and set it on the TV stand behind them.

"Lay down," Diamond whispered. Her soft request was the total opposite of her intense gaze.

Jessica took a step back and jumped on top of the bed backwards. She scooted further away from the edge, never breaking her stare in the process.

Diamond wasted no time chasing her. She slowly climbed on top of the bed, then on top of Jessica. Jessica wasn't drunk, but she was lax enough to allow her best friend to explore her body as if they were one. Diamond and Jessica lay body to body on top of the sheets. Diamond smiled and briefly pressed her lips to

Jessica's, kissing them softy. The anticipation had Jessica in a state of bliss. She bit her bottom lip to keep from smiling as much as she wanted to smile at the moment.

Diamond took Jessica's lip into her mouth, pulling it away from her teeth. She sucked it for a few seconds, then released it. Diamond moves down to her breast. She covered as much as she could with her mouth, using her tongue to circle the nipple. She rotated, moving to the other breast. She reached down and slid her finger in between Jessica thighs. Her pussy resembled a cave. Warm and moist.

Jessica had never been with a woman before, and although it was her best friend, she didn't want to miss it by keeping her eyes closed. Diamond watched Jessica's body with the same fascination as her hand glided across her stomach, then moved down her until she reaches her thighs. She pushed her legs apart and gazed down at Jessica's perfectly shaved and plump pussy. Her pink center glistened from the creamy juices that clothed her cave. Watching Diamond as she watched her in enthrallment was a turn-on for Jessica alone. Two of her fingers slid into her, and it instantly made her lids heavy. Jessica realized right then that watching Diamond wouldn't be such an easy task.

Her thumb remained on the outside of Jessica, teasing every spot it could touch. Jessica moaned, then her eyes closed. She instantly found her button. She attacked her clit, but in a gentle way. Jessica prayed she didn't stop. With her fingers still inside, she eased up. Her mouth found Jessica's. Her tongue went down Jessica's throat. She curved her fingers upwards to stimulate her G-spot.

Shit.

Her mouth slowly began to explore its way down Jessica's chin, then the dip to her throat. Her lips glided down her chest, covered her nipple, down her stomach. Jessica's stomach quivered and her breath quickened. She settles herself between Jessica's legs, again.

Diamond's mouth covered her opening, causing Jessica's back to arch and heart to race. This time, Diamond had her button with a bit more pressure. Jessica relaxed. She didn't even care that she was moaning so loudly that if Parlay pulled up right now, he'd hear her all the way in the driveway. She was digging her heels into the mattress, trying to scoot backwards towards the headboard, because it was too much for her. Diamond eased her fingers out and grabbed Jessica by the hips and held her against her mouth. She knew she was about to bust and she refused to let her climb away. Jessica's legs began to shudder. Diamond slid her fingers back inside of her cave. Jessica reached above her head and grabbed a pillow, because she was certain she was going to awake the neighbors with the scream that she desperately tried to subdue, but not for long. Suddenly she felt like she was floating.

"I'm 'bout to——" she whispered and bit down on her lips so hard she was sure she buried it. "I'm cum—— Jessica released before she could complete her sentence. Her body felt so lax, like she had melted to the bed.

Diamond took the pillow off her face and tossed it to the side. "Now go get in the shower before Lay comes."

Diamond was gone. The lights were dimmed and the candles were lit when Parlay arrived. Jessica had just placed the silverware on the table next to the covered plates when he walked through the door. Her ass cheeks hung out the bottom of the satin robe as she strutted out of the kitchen and into the living area. She still felt the drink from earlier.

"Hey bae," Parlay announced, locking the door.

"I missed you, zaddy."

Parlay held her tightly. "I missed you too, ma." He leaned down and kissed the top of her head.

Jessica grabbed two of his fingers and led him to the table. Parlay's stomach growled and his eyes glistened at the sight of it. "Check you out." He smiled in awe, pulling both chairs away from the table and taking a seat. Parlay tried to mentally figure out the occasion before asking. If it was something significant, his failure to remember would surely upset her.

They ate in silence. Guilt abruptly enveloped Jessica.

Parlay, on the other hand, was still racking his brain but devouring the great meal in the midst of it.

How could she fuck her best friend in the same bed she lay in every night with the man she exchanged vows with? Jessica didn't know if her drunken state intensified the pressure of the guilt, but she was beginning to feel cornered. *I should tell him in case he finds out.*

Parlay belched loudly, stealing Jessica's attention from the thoughts that ran rapidly inside of her head. He gave up. "So." He placed his elbows on the table. "What's the occasion?"

True enough, her mother's birthday was tomorrow, but that wasn't the reason for the festivities. She wanted some dick. The little voice in her head thought otherwise. She eased to her feet and hovered over him. Parlay peered at her. She wrapped her arms around his neck. Her skin smelled like warm French vanilla. He stuck his nose directly in between her perky C-cup breasts savoring her scent. His hand slowly glided up and down the back of her leg. Parlay moved his legs from underneath the table. Jessica now positioned herself between his legs. His hands slowly trailed all the way up her back until he touched the back of her neck.

The simple gesture alone sent Jessica's hormones into a frenzy. She needed some dick. The orgasm Diamond had given her was the best release she ever had from oral pleasure. But that was just the appetizer. She needed the main course, which was some long, hard steel. She needed Parlay. He tightened his grip on Jessica's neck and forced her head towards his until their mouths collided, caressed, and clashed. Parlay began to stand, but his mouth stayed on Jessica's. He walked her a few feet away from the table until her back is against the wall.

Both of their mouths were overly possessive as if there was some sort of competition. Parlay's hands fell to Jessica's waist. Moans and grunts fill the room. Jessica unbuttoned his Prada jeans. She tugged at one side while he tugged at the other. They fell to the floor. There was a bulge in his Ethika briefs, but it wasn't trying to tear through the costly cloth like it had done the night before.

Her mood shifted and a cloud of defeat suddenly hovered over her. They were on two different levels. She was soaked, her juices trinkling down her thighs. Parlay, on the other hand, was everything other than stiff. His hand moved from her waist down to her leg. He lifted Jessica's leg up, wrapped it around him, then pressed against her passionately. Tears filled her eyes as she moaned into his mouth.

Jessica wanted to be sexed. She deserved to be sexed. Their kiss stop abruptly, but it was not Jessica who was pulling away. It was Parlay. He dropped her leg and uses his hand to lean against the wall in case he needed any support to stand. Fear surged through Jessica, afraid that she may have spoken her thoughts aloud and Parlay heard her, but that wasn't the case.

Parlay pressed his forehead against the wall beside her head, still leaning against her as the both of them stood quietly. Seconds passed and he finally pushed off the wall, turned around, and walked away.

"I don't know what's going on, Jess, and I deeply apologize for making you suffer too," he apologized, but his tone lack sincerity. It was as insipid as eating cardboard box, bland and rehearsed as if he was being forced.

Jessica wanted to speak, but a cluster of emotions was caught in her throat.

He adjusted his nuts and veered to the left towards the bed-room, leaving Jessica against the wall in the living room alone.

S. Hawkins

Chapter 14
Epitome of a Nympho

Jessica awakened to an empty bed the next day. The sunshine through the transparent blinds forced her to peek around swiftly. Panic instantly overloaded her as she remembered the altercation with her and Parlay last night. Sure enough, she wished Parlay's dick could harden whenever he was aroused, but it wasn't a good enough reason to abandon their marriage. *Period.*

What disturbed Jessica was wondering if Parlay felt that way too. She listened for a sound indicating Parlay's presence. She heard nothing, so she climbed out of bed and moved towards the door.

The delicious aroma collided with her nostrils instantly. Hope filled her eyes as a slow smile spread across her face. The muscles in his perfectly sculpted back twitched as he lightly shook the pan. She climbed up on the stool. Disappointment filled her as she desperately coaxed herself into losing the attraction that abruptly surfaced every time she saw her husband. She moved the strands of hair behind her ear, then cleared her throat. Parlay turned around swiftly.

"It smells good in here," Jessica admitted as soon as they locked eyes.

"Anything for you, love," he responded. A slow smile spread across his face, yet his eyes were full of mischief.

Jessica smiled back, pretending not to notice. It was too early for an argument. "I made blueberry pancakes, hash browns, eggs, and bacon. Are you ready to eat?" he asked, holding a maroon spatula in one hand and a protein shake in the other.

Unbeknownst to Jessica, Parlay was awakened hours ago. Obnoxious shrieking and awful cries invaded his mental in the wee hours of the night, forcing him out of his deep slumber. His medication eventually gave him enough tranquility to silence the monsters inside of his head. What he found the most frightening was those same monsters were his family, only in a gruesome form. An image that would've bought a smile to his face years ago made him quiver in fear today.

"I'll set up the table," Jessica offered.

Parlay made the plates. They ate in silence. Their eyes were their only form of communication. However, it was like trying to peek through fog. It was simply incomprehensible. Jessica picked at her food. Parlay devoured his.

The sound of Parlay's phone ringing grabbed both of their attention. His face scrunched in confusion. He involuntarily peeked up at Jessica, then swiftly peeked back down at his screen. It was Natasha. If he didn't answer, questions would surely arise, so he did.

Natasha's voice was raspy and weak. "Lay, I need you."

Parlay pushed away from the table. "Where are you?" Jessica looked at him with curiosity.

"I'm in the hospital."

"Bet." Parlay ended the call and jumped to his feet. He knew Jessica was about to question him, so he beat her to it. "Prime's in some trouble. I'm about to go see what's up and I'll call you as soon as I get shit figured out."

Jessica nodded and Parlay took off towards the bedroom.

***

Parlay arrived at the airport in Atlanta before sunset. He pulled out his phone to call Prime.

"Hello?"

"Look to your left, fam, I'm right here," Prime responded. He sat in his Escalade watching Parlay from a distance. He didn't phone him sooner because that would've meant missing out on the amazing release.

Genesis wiped the corners of her mouth and climbed over the middle console and into the backseat. Prime stuffed his meat inside of his briefs and pulled up his Nike shorts.

"Come here," he requested, turning around in his seat.

Genesis leaned in and he pressed his soft, wet lips against hers. Since the minute he arrived in ATL, they lived every second like it was a special occasion. Club hopping, shopping, fine dining, spas, and amazing sex. Prime introduced her to the best weed she ever smoked. In just a few weeks of knowing her, he had captured her mind, body, and soul. His dick was as potent as heroin, and for that reason alone, several bags and cases of her belongings were piled up in the rear of the truck. She refused to endure the withdrawal.

Parlay opened the door to the backseat, ready to toss his small duffel bag inside. He paused mid-swing, spotting Genesis. "Shit, my bad." He handed it to her instead. "Set this beside you for me," he said, before closing the door. "Y'all alright?" Parlay asked, wading into the passenger seat. He was relieved to be behind the tint instead of outside in the blistering heat.

"Hell yeah, ready to head back to the city tomorrow." Genesis leaned forward, gripping the back of Parlay's headrest.

"I'm going to the city too." She grinned, exposing her pearly whites. She was elated.

Parlay slightly turned and said, "That's what's up." He handed Prime his phone after activating the GPS. Prime eased away from the curb.

"I'm sorry 'bout your friend. They say dude beat her down at the restaurant."

Parlay's nostrils flared as he gritted his teeth. He did so to refrain from expressing how he really felt and expose the feelings he still had bottled inside for Natasha. "That's some pussy shit, but that's her business. I'm just here to see about her because she asked," Parlay admitted, portraying himself as unbothered.

"You leaving with us tomorrow, right?" Prime asked.

"That's fine. The flight had me a little shook anyways. Besides, I don't like when my ears start popping and shit."

Everyone erupted in laughter. Shortly, they pulled into the spacious lot of the hospital.

"Where y'all about to run off to?" Parlay asked while unbuckling the seatbelt.

"Grab something to eat and get a room for the night," Prime answered, turning around and gazing at Genesis. She sat on the edge of the seat, eager to climb to the front.

Parlay slightly chuckled before climbing out of the truck. "I'll call you," he voiced, then closed the door.

He strolled into the hospital. Checking in was easier than what he thought. Obviously, Natasha had informed more than one person of his arrival. The elevator was directly across from the room she was assigned to. He sighed deeply before pushing his way inside.

Immediately, he spotted Natasha lying there motionless. From a distance, she didn't appear as grim as he thought. He moved closer. His breaths were shallow and the pounding in his chest was as pestering as the voices in his head.

A cluster of knots adorned her forehead. A wave of heat swept over him. He clutched his stomach and pressed his lips together to withhold the contents that threatened to let loose. Her eyes were black and the darkest shade of purple Parlay had ever seen. Two, maybe three stitches, were weaved into her face merely a few inches above her left brow.

Natasha's eyes fluttered open. "I felt you," she said in a whisper-like tone. She opened her eyes completely and eased backwards until she was sitting up.

"Whoa, whoa, whoa." Parlay held his hands out. She was moving too quick for her own good.

"Lay, I'm fine. I've been in here two days already, so I've healed a little bit," she spoke in between wincing.

Parlay's eyes narrowed into slits as he leaned as close as possible against the rail. She may have been battered and bruised, but her beauty shined through like a ray of light in the tunnel. She placed her hand on top of his and chills traveled down his spine as he swallowed the baby lump that formed in his throat.

Old love was like old money. It was definite when everything else was skeptical.

"Tell me what happened?" he asked, yet it sounded more like a demand.

I'd really like to know what happened to us? The thought emerged instantly, but Natasha lacked the courage to voice it. Truthfully, she had loved Parlay many days and nights, but the plights of life intervened, making it strenuous for the two to keep a firm grip on something that only they believed and desired. She waited every day for Parlay to reach out like some sort of ghetto Cinderella, but it never happened. Weirdly, things consumed her and just like most women, she yearned for everything she desired and a number of things she disdained. Several trips to the hospital was one of them. Tears streamed down her face and dripped onto her chest. She locked eyes with Parlay.

"Well…" she paused. "I would tell you you're the reason for this." She paused again. "But you're not. He enjoys kicking my ass and he been wanting to for so long. He just needed something to justify it so he'd have a probable argument once I threatened to leave his ass." Her lips quivered as she opened her mouth to speak, but nothing came out.

Parlay lowered his head. Shame and guilt consumed him. "I'm sorry you had——"

"I've been getting my ass kicked for so long I should be used to it by now," Natasha confessed, ceasing his speech.

"How long you been going through this. Why you haven't said anything?" Parlay asked. He gripped the rail so tight veins protruded from his hand.

"He's got damn near the whole city sowed. Who am I going to tell? These been his streets! I'm the foreigner out here. I left my city years ago!" She jabbed her chest with her index finger. "We've been married since October 6, 2020. I met him in 2019."

"So y'all jumped the broom——" Parlay paused as the familiar day surfaced repeatedly in his mental like some sort of alarm. He mouthed the date repeatedly as he began to pace the room. Perhaps he could be tripping and the date wasn't as significant as he made it out to be, but something in the pit of his soul said otherwise.

"Parlay," Natasha called out.

"Huh?" he mumbled, steady pacing back and forth. An image of a teary-eyed Jessica suddenly emerged. His movement ceased and so did his breathing. The constant sound from the heart monitor absolutely clung to him like a layer of clothing.

"Parlay?" Natasha called out again.

He could hear the distress. He walked back to her bed.

"My bad. My mind went somewhere else. You hungry?" Parlay asked in an attempt to divert his attention.

"I'm fine, as long as you here." She reached out and grabbed his hand.

He covered hers with his and firmly gripped it. Inwardly, he was cursing himself for being so forgetful, but he couldn't deny the electricity that surged through him every time they locked eyes or made physical contact.

"For sho'."

Parlay continued to pry whenever Natasha would snap him out of the deep trance he was in. Mentally, he was in shambles. He wanted to stand with Natasha and assist her with ridding the demons of her past, but he needed to be home so that he could ease the mental anguish and emotional trauma that Jessica dealt with every year around this time. However, Natasha's wound was fresh. It had been years since Jessica's mother died. He wished he could take a journey through both of their hearts to see who needed him more.

"Lay, I need you." She paused. "Even if it's just for the night."

S. Hawkins

Chapter 15
Can't Help but Wait

Meanwhile, back in Dallas, Jessica lay curled up on the couch, tears soaking her face. She had been staring at the screen since Parlay left, hoping he'd call at any second and announce his return. She read the closed captions as the news anchor announced the weather report. There was a heavy chance of a thunderstorm, which only deepened her depression. She needed him, especially before the day turned into night and she would have to lie in bed alone, listening to the silence. Jessica's phone vibrated and she almost dropped it trying to grab it off the table next to her. It was a text from Jah.

Can we go somewhere and chill?

Jessica replied instantly. *I'm really not feeling it.*

She laid the phone down against her chest and closed her eyes. The constant crying had swollen her lids, making them feel heavier than usual.

Come on, if you decide to meet up with me, I promise I can lift your spirits.

A half smile etched her face. She wiped her face clean with the back of her hand and sat completely up on the couch, reclining against the pillow.

OK. Let me get myself together. What time and place?

Jessica stood to her feet and stretched her arms out toward the ceiling. She straightened the pillows on the sofa and began to undress, tossing her pajamas on the floor along the way.

At six. I'll drop the location in a few.

Jessica looked at the time. It was about five minutes after five, so she didn't have long. She rushed to her bedroom, her eyes fastened on the scenery outside of her window. It was darker than usual. She stepped closer. Grey clouds decorated the sky, resembling some sort of odd pattern.

Please don't rain. She took off towards the bathroom. Jessica quickly freshened up and got dressed. She chose something cute, but simple, a pair of denim high waist jeans and an oversized crop top sweater. She threw her hair up in a bun precisely, perfecting her baby hairs that lay neatly on her forehead.

Boom! Boom!

Her windows rattled a bit as the thundering announced its arrival. Jessica froze in fear. Suddenly, raindrops slammed against her window pane. It was so loud and sharp it could've easily been mistaken for hail. Her shoulders slumped in defeat. She dragged to the living room and pulled aside the long and thick curtains that separated her from her patio. It was pouring down with no chances of easing up.

She moved closer to the edge and leaned against the brick wall as she peered out into the sky and watched the rain fall. Jessica smacked her lips and removed the phone from her bra. Instead of texting, she called Jah.

Her raspy voice blurred through the speaker. "What's up?" she asked. Her words dripped with dread. It was like she knew what Jessica was about to say.

Jessica hesitated a bit. "Um, look, it's raining cats and dogs. Let's just reschedule and chill another day."

"Alright, bet," Jah blurted, barely allowing Jessica to finish her statement.

The dial tone chimed in. Jessica pulled the phone away from her ear, stunned. She shrugged, then tossed her phone on the sofa. She stared around the empty living room. If only Parlay was home. She undressed and changed into something a bit more comfortable. She retrieved a wooden spoon from the drawer and grabbed the gallon of Oatmeal pie ice cream from the freezer.

I'll just eat away my depression and binge watch P. Valley.

She hadn't spoken to Diamond since yesterday. It felt like so many days had passed in between, but it was just yesterday. She considered calling her, but she knew it would be awkward as hell. Too awkward. And then they would end up having sex. That wasn't a good habit to start, and she planned on breaking it before it began. It happened. They enjoyed it, and that was it.

Jessica repeatedly dug into the container with her eyes fastened on the screen. Involuntarily, her mind drifted off to a memory of her and her mother, one she would never forget. She muted the TV and closed the lid on the ice cream. She chuckled and began rocking back and forth as she concentrated on trying to relive the piece of memory she did recall. She cried silent tears. It was silent minus the chuckling. It was a mixture of joyful tears and tears of heartbreak. The what if's arose, increasing her state of gloom.

The doorbell sounded and everything ceased. Her tears, the rocking, the memory she tried her damndest to recall. She jumped to her feet, cleaning her face as she moved to the door. She stood on the tips of her toes and peered out the peephole, but drops of rain had clung to it, blurring the presence on the other side of the door. Whoever it was had some kind of bags in their hand. She unlocked the locks. Her brows dipped and her mouth slightly opened, but nothing came out.

Jah cleared her throat. Water dripped from her hair and every article of clothing. "You just gon' leave me out here like this?"

Jessica snapped out of the daze she was in and stood to the side.

Jah scurried inside and immediately set the bags down. She peered around. Her eyes fell on the patio. "That's a patio, right?"

Jessica nodded her head. Jah's presence definitely stunned her, leaving her at a loss for words. Jah rushed out onto the patio. Jessica removed the food from the bags and placed the food on the table. She peered around swiftly for anything out of place. Jah stepped back inside with nothing but her sports bra and briefs on. Her hair, her chiseled abs, toned arms, thighs, and calves glistened. "I wrung my clothes out and hung them on your wall out there," she said, pointing behind her.

Jessica tried desperately not to stare. She dropped her head. "I'll go get them and toss them in the dryer." She vanished in a hurry.

Jah walked inside the kitchen and grabbed a few paper towels to dry her damp skin.

"I would've gave you a towel," Jessica admitted from a distance.

"It's cool," Jah responded before balling up the napkins and trashing them. She followed behind Jessica slowly as she led the way to the sofa, assaulting her with her eyes every step of the way. Everything about Jessica was arousing to Jah: her walk, the sway of her hips, the natural arch of her back, the slenderness in her neck and even the way she raked her fingers through her hair whenever she was nervous. She sat on the sofa Indian style and faced Jah's direction. Jah followed suit, her long legs gapped open and her arms draped along the edge of the multicolored sectional. Lust draped her eyes, forcing Jessica to fidget with the buttons on her shirt. Jah's hard gaze was very intimidating and demanding. It was arousing, but a bit unpleasant as well. Perhaps, Jessica wasn't used to a set of eyes that stared right through her, making her feel transparent as water. Her expensive cologne was as potent as her as her gaze.

"Why you come?" Jessica asked softly, peering down at her hands.

"Well, honestly…" Jah paused turning to face her. She lifted Jessica's chin with her finger. Jessica desperately wanted to look away but she held her gaze instead. "Well, I can relate to the level of pain you're feeling today. If I can do anything to suppress it and simply put a smile on your face, I'll do it. Just tell me what to do," Jah spoke her eyes fastened on Jessica's.

Tears filled Jessica's almond-shaped eyes. Jah hadn't known her a month, yet she was willing to help carry the load of burdens that had weighed Jessica down for years.

Jah placed her hand on Jessica's cheek and with a stroke of her thumb, she swiped the tear away. She held her breath so she wouldn't cry with her. Jessica opened her mouth to speak, but Jah silenced her with a kiss. More tears fell.

This should be Parlay. He's supposed to be here. Not Jah.

"I can't believe you remembered," Jessica whined in between sobs.

"Shhh," Jah whispered, placing a finger up to Jessica lips.

She immediately stopped crying, but the sniffling continued. Jah's finger slid softly down her mouth and chin. Her eyes followed the tip of her finger as it continued to move, trailing gently down her throat, to her chest, and further down to her stomach. That potency of the finger was equivalent to ten. It was quite odd since it wasn't even making contact with her skin. Her entire hand replaced her finger as she slightly traced her stomach over the top of her shirt. Jah's hands swiftly moved to the back of her head and she pressed her mouth to Jessica's hard and passionately. Jah pressed forward until Jessica's back was against the arm of the couch. She slid her silk shorts and underwear down at the same time as Jessica hooked her thumbs onto the hips of Jah briefs and pushed them down.

Jessica watched Jah in amazement as she reached behind the pillow on the sofa and pulled out her toy. She wanted to touch it, it looked so authentic. It even had a vein – two, to be exact. It was about two shades darker than Jah, but the size is what made Jessica's pussy pit-a-pat. She quickly secured the penis in position. If Jessica wouldn't have seen the entire transaction, she would've surely thought Jah was born with it. She curled her finger, signaling for Jessica to come her way. Jessica eased off the sofa, her plump pussy on full display.

"Lay down."

Jessica laid down and Jah eased on top of her. Jah took both of Jessica's hands and moving them above her head, she pressed them to the floor. She drop her forehead to hers and they kissed. Jessica kissed Jah desperately, furiously filling Jah's mouth with the taste of her tears. She closed her eyes to cease them from flowing. Jah kept hers open. Jessica's pain and vulnerability aroused her even more, swelling the throbbing button between her legs. Jah slowly pushed herself between Jessica legs, spreading them wider. She kissed her on the neck as she eased her hand to the stiffness between her legs.

The perfect round tip grazed Jessica's center, then her clit. Jessica shuddered beneath Jah. Without warning, Jah slid into her slowly. Jessica exhaled once Jah was completely inside, each of them taking the other's mind away from whatever their pain stemmed from. Jah pulled out and then thrust inside her again, this time with everything she had. The pain predominated over the pleasure. It was evident she was hurting too.

Give me all of that shit, Jah.

"Damn, Jessica," she whispered. "Give me all of it. I need all of it," Jah continued.

Appalled, Jessica's mouth fell open. Her body stilled beneath Jah's upon realizing what she said. Jessica wrapped her hand around the back of Jah's head and pulled her mouth to hers. She moaned inside of Jessica's mouth. Her eyes remain focused on Jessica's the entire time she moved in and out of her. Jessica closed her eyes, hoping she could conceal her pain like she could conceal her irises. It was too late. Everything was out in the open. There was nothing left to hide. Jah could convey hers and she could convey Jah's. If it wasn't her eyes that unveiled her feelings, Jessica could certainly decipher them according to her thrusts.

"Don't stop," Jessica begged, becoming more possessed the longer Jah was inside of her.

"Oh, I'm not." Jah applied more pressure. She grabbed her leg behind the knee and pulled it up between their chests, then entered her from a slightly different angle. She held her leg firmly against her shoulder and thrust into her even deeper.

"Jah! Oh my God," she moaned. She began to shudder beneath her.

Somehow, Jah dropped her legs or they magically fell and their mouths meet. They kissed as hard and deep as the strokes she hitting her with.

"Fuck!" Jah yelled.

Jessica was shaking and Jah was panting. Jah pushed into her again and held her firmly against the floor with her weight. She thrust again, harder this time, so hard Jessica scooted away from her, so she slid her arms under her shoulders and cupped her hands upwards, holding her in one place as she repeatedly pushed into her. Hard, long, deep strokes that drew moans out of both them.

"Yeah, Jah, fuck me harder!" she begged.

Jah thrust harder.

Jessica squeezed her ass cheeks.

Jah moved faster.

They both gasped for air. It was the most intense sex either of them had ever had. Jessica wailed loudly before going limp and Jah gave one last thrust before her body stilled.

"Jessica," she said, moaning her name against her mouth as her body recovered from the massive release. "Fuck." Jah slowly pulled out and lay her head against Jessica chest.

"Huh?" Jessica responded weakly.

"Aye, I don't know what you gon' do." She sat up on her elbows. "But that right there…" She pointed to her pussy that glistened from the combination of juices that sloppily coated it. "I need that, gots to have it. It's mine now."

Jessica attempted to chuckle nervously, but the fluttering in her chest was a sure sign that Jah possessed zero humor.

"Alright, I'm telling you what," she stated, her eyes locked hard with Jessica's.

The ringing of her phone diverted both of their attention. Jah still appeared unbothered. Jessica looked shocked. She quickly dashed for her phone. Her eyes widened as soon as Parlay's name flashed across the screen.

"Hurry, go get dressed. My room is the last one at the end of the hallway. Hurry!" Jessica voiced with urgency.

Jah didn't flinch at first, but she finally did as she was told. There was no need for bucking now. She knew what it was when she signed up. Before turning around and walking away, Jah's piercing eyes burned holes in the center of her face.

"Hello?" Jessica answered, afraid of what was about to spew from Parlay's mouth.

"Bae, come pick me up from the airport."

Jessica covered the receiver and sighed deeply. "DFW?"

"Yeah."

Jessica scurried to her feet and ended the call. "Jah!" she yelled, moving towards her direction.

Jah was walking out of her room and Jessica was entering. She bypassed Jah and into the bathroom. She turned on the water, wrung out the washcloth, and carefully wiped her pussy. She peered up and caught Jah's harsh gaze. Jah had seen enough.

Jessica dropped her head. Guilt weakened her gaze. She peered up seconds later and this time, the only eyes she locked with was her own. Jah had left. She hung the towel over the rail and rushed back into the living room. She peered out the window and watched Jah's taillights until they were no longer in view. She quickly straightened up any and everything that appeared out of place, then threw on the same thing she had in before Jah stripped her out of them.

***

Jessica spotted Parlay standing underneath the ramp. He had been patiently waiting on her. He kissed her on the lips and then her cheek as soon as he climbed in. He carelessly tossed his bag into the backseat.

Jessica questioned him as soon as the door closed shut. "Why are you at the airport, and where is Prime?"

Parlay rolled his eyes and sighed deeply. He pondered on answering the question. If it was any other day, he wouldn't have. He would make an exception for today. The least he could do was lie because she definitely wasn't going to get the truth.

"I had to make a last-minute pick up. Prime got locked up. That's why I'm here alone and needed a ride." The lie fell from his lips so smoothly that anyone with ears wouldn't have second guessed him.

Jessica hit the brakes. She and Parlay jerked forward. "Are you serious?" she asked. Fear paired with bewilderment as their eyes locked.

Parlay nodded in response. He didn't have the energy to repeat it.

"What happened, Lay?" she pried, concern lacing her words She searched his eyes as if they held the answer to her question.

"He good, bae. Come on," Parlay urged, then pinched the bridge of his nose.

Jessica pursed her lips as if she was about to speak, but she was all too familiar with the small gesture. Whenever Parlay did it, he was either extremely upset or irritated, so she held back the concerns that emerged. He needed peace of mind. She was going to give him that instead of disturb it. She would only speak if asked.

Jessica lagged behind Parlay as he made his way up the driveway. She moved like she had the weight of the world on her shoulders.

Unbeknownst to her, Parlay felt the same way. The silence was as pestering as a steady clamor. He unlocked the door and walked slowly through his home. He looked more like a tourist instead of the owner. He paused. The strong whiff assaulted his nostrils. The scent that lingered on his mouth from Jessica matched the scent that lingered around his home. However, it began to wither the further he walked into his home.

Jessica eyed him suspiciously. She didn't know if she should speak or remain speechless, without appearing suspect. Parlay tried masking the obvious, but Jessica's guilt had given her a keen eye to spot anything out of the ordinary. She followed close behind, trying to appear uninterested, but she was as nervous as a guilty man on the day of sentencing. Parlay was bothered, yet he concealed it well. He was curious. He wanted to ask, but it was senseless since a lie wasn't anything to a pair of lips to tell.

Jessica held her breath as Parlay opened the door to the bedroom. She was hoping like hell Jah didn't leave anything behind. He took everything out of his pocket and tossed it in the bed along with his duffel bag. He began stripping out of his clothes. His strong physique forced Jessica to swallow the lump in her throat. There it was again: the predominating guilt that ascended from the pit of her stomach like acid reflux. She lowered her head and moved around him. She swiftly tossed the keys on the nightstand and climbed into bed in the material she was clad in. Parlay moved to the shower, not paying Jessica any attention whatsoever.

The steaming hot water was like a breath of fresh air to Parlay. He imagined the water removing the debris and the oath that kept him tied to the woman in the next room. Feelings, in spite of how faint they were, were indeed valid, yet they were diminishing by the day.

A terror-stricken scream brought Parlay down to one knee. He covered his ears in an attempt to cease the noise only he could her. "Aarrghh!" he sounded.

Jessica jolted up from the fetal position she was laying in and scurried to the bathroom. She burst through the door and to his side. On one knee, she and Parlay were eye level. His eyes were fixed on the ground beneath him as he rocked, tightly gripping his ears. Jessica peered in bewilderment. It had been a minute since he had an episode. She instantly assumed it was her fault since she had requested he stop taking his medicine. She wanted to console him.

He wanted to deal with his issues alone. He knew he chose the wrong one to console the moment he climbed into Jessica's car. However, the second he said "I do", it disabled him from thinking and acting selfishly. He made the mental decision to hold himself accountable, even if she didn't.

"My medication is inside the bag on the bed," he voiced in between wincing.

Jessica quickly went to retrieve it. Parlay took advantage of the temporary silence and began getting dressed. He grabbed the damp washcloth off the rack and turned to peer at his reflection as he washed his face. As he dragged the cloth from his cheek and over his nose, the familiar smell caused him to stiffen. Nothing moved but his thick brows as they dipped in confusion.

Pussy, her pussy, tampered pussy.

It was fresh, minus a bit of a stench - a stench of sweat; sweaty sex. He slightly balled up the towel and pressed it against his nose. He deeply inhaled.

Jessica scurried inside but halted as she watched her husband savor her scent. Unbeknownst to her, he was actually taking the time to remember where they started and the place they were at now. Parlay had done many things, but cheating wasn't one of them. She had been fucking another man in the house they shared. She even went to the lengths of attempting to cover it up. Infidelity predominated any vows. It was completely unacceptable, in Parlay's perspective. He lowered his hand from his nose as his arm fell by his side. His head swiveled in Jessica's direction. Fear covered her face like the best Sephora foundation.

Confirmation.

Even if her guilt wasn't as evident, Parlay was far from a fool. He knew Jessica as well as he knew himself. He just pretended to not know sometimes, because if he made it known that he knew, situations would have to be addressed, and he simply didn't have the time nor energy to do so. Therefore, he acted oblivious to a lot. He stretched out his arm and held out his empty hand. He knew that his silence was driving Jessica crazy. She dropped the bottle into his hand. It was nearly empty. He held it up and shook it. There was just four left.

"Thank you," he said. His eyes were vacant as an abandoned lot, and hard as a sofa without pillows.

Jessica was hoping he said something, anything to confirm that she had been caught so that she could use that opportunity to secure him in her bed of lies. Yet Parlay did the exact opposite.

"That's all I wanted," he voiced and began moving around the bathroom.

Jessica left. She needed to breathe. The door to the bathroom opened. She swiftly grabbed her scarf off the dresser and wrapped it around her head. She and Parlay locked eyes through the mirror that sat atop of the dresser. She swallowed the lump in her throat as she felt that button between her legs start to throb. Shirtless, wearing just a pair of briefs and Polo sweats, he was breathtaking.

"Have you seen my other script?" he asked, holding up the now-empty bottle.

Jessica scanned her dresser. She had remembered seeing it there earlier. "I, I thought——" she stammered in a low tone. "No, I, um, I haven't."

Parlay moved towards the night stand and placed that empty one on top of it. "It's probably out there in my car, I'll go look for it in the morning," he said, yanking the covers back.

Chapter 16
Just Can't Let Go

Jessica awoke the next morning to an empty bed. The room wasn't empty, so she didn't panic. She had a feeling he would leave early so that he could work on getting Prime out of whatever situation that he was in. She reached underneath her pillow and grabbed her phone. It was dead. She cursed, then quickly rolled out of bed and placed it on the charger.

She had scrolled up and down her Facebook and Instagram pages all night, crying silent tears until she fell asleep. Parlay had given her his back from the moment he climbed onto the California King.

The sound of the doorbell directed her attention. She was clueless on who it could be. She figured it was Diamond. They hadn't spoken in days and if she had been trying to contact her and not getting an answer, she would surely pop up. She undid the locks and swung the door open. It was Jah. Frightened, her eyes grew twice their size as she peered behind her. "You can't be here right now. My husband left to grab something and he will be back any minute," she spoke quickly.

"I'll just go out the back. My car parked three houses down," Jah pleaded. Although her joy had vanished the moment the word "husband" fell from Jessica's lips, it wasn't effective enough to make her leave. She needed to see her, touch her, feel her any or all of the above.

Jessica peered around once more before pulling Jah inside. She couldn't resist the chick. There was something about the way her eyes lingered daringly, boldly, that turned her on. Her walk, the way she dressed, her self-assurance, and selfless personality.

Jah stepped inside and Jessica locked the doors behind her. As soon as the lock clicked, Jah turned to face her and Jessica was on her before she could even blink. They kissed like they had been apart for years. Moans and grunts filled the living room. Neither of them stopped to breathe. Jessica pulled away.

"Let's go to my room. Just in case he comes back, you can hop out my window."

Jah bit her tongue and nodded. Something was going to have to give. Sooner rather than later.

Jessica led the way, holding on to Jah's finger instead of her hand. Jah watched her ass the entire time as they moved down the long hallway. She bit her lip in anticipation. Jessica reached for the light switch, but Jah grabbed her hand. Jessica gasped and peered at her over her shoulder. "What are you doing?" she asked in a submissive tone.

"You want to sneak; let's sneak. No lights, no noises." Jah pressed her soft, juicy lips against hers. "Pretend we teenagers again inside of our mom's house and we're being as cautious as possible 'cause we're aware of the harsh consequences," Jah spoke in between pecks.

"Okay," Jessica whispered into her mouth.

Jah helped her peel off her top. Her breasts hung freely underneath. Jah bit her lip and pinched Jessica nipple at the same time. Her mouth watered in anticipation. She wanted more of Jessica the second she was away from her. A hissing sound escaped Jessica lips as she shimmied out of the silk pajamas shorts. Jah lifted her chin and they kissed savagely. Jah pulled back.

"Hold on," Jah said.

She quickly removed her clothes and set them in a pile on side of the door. Instead of being slightly ajar, she opened the door halfway.

"Just in case we don't hear him pull up we can hear the locks turning."

There was a speck of light from the hallway. Jessica nodded and Jah leaned into her personal space. Something hard jabbed her midsection. Instinctively she grabbed it. Her heart fluttered, her breath ceased and her pussy moistened simultaneously. She thought Jah had forgotten it.

Jah's gaze was intense as she peered at Jessica while pecking her lips slow and passionately. She slid her hand in between her thighs and in between the soft, plump lips that barricade the entry of her tunnel. Her wetness effortlessly coated her fingers, sending Jah into a frenzy. She moved her fingers around and between her lips, then started attacking her button. Jessica's legs shook as she stood there taking the pleasurable beating.

Jah grabbed the back of her head with the other hand and pulled her into a long, tongue-wrestling kiss. Unable to hold out anymore, she lifted Jessica off her desk and laid her on the edge of the bed. She forced Jessica's legs open, causing a sigh of pleasure to escape from her mouth. She quickly covered her mouth to conceal it. Jah pulled her closer off the edge by her waist. She pulled her again until the stiffness between her legs poked Jessica's box. She slid in without warning.

A muffled scream filled the room. Jah keep digging, shifting like she was a surfboard and rolling like she was in ATL at Cascades on a Sunday night. Breathing, whimpering and macaroni being stirred were the only sounds in the two-story home. She slid out and thrust forward. She did it again, harder this time.

Jessica eyes widened as she felt Jah's finger knocking at her back door. She felt around for her arm, but before she could grip it, she had already slid her finger inside. It was small, but not too small. She assumed it was her thumb. Jah gave her short, quick strokes, her finger mimicking the rhythm. Jessica squeezed her eyes shut as she tightened her pussy around the pole inside of her. She didn't know if she was going or coming, and she didn't care as long as Jah was still inside of her once she arrived. She spread one of her cheeks with her free hand and leaned down and bit her quick and hard in the inside of her thigh. Jessica tightened her legs as she released a quick, breathless scream.

"Cum for me," Jah whispered, thrusting harder.

Jessica lifted and rotated her hips, squeezing and massaging her breasts, enjoying the moments of bliss. Sex with Jah was so different and refreshing.

Jah felt the vibration of Jessica's legs and she knew at any second, she would erupt like a volcano. She pulled out and pushed her legs all the way back. "Hold them," she demanded before leaning down.

As soon as her breath grazed her pussy, Jessica melted into the sheets. Jah covered her opening with her warm and wet mouth. She slurped her clean of her juices, slid her thick tongue up and down each of her lips. She attacked her button. Her tongue swiftly flickered across it, up and down it, then she slowly pressed further against her button and circled it.

"Ooohh, Jah, please!" she cried.

Jah remained persistent and it wasn't long before Jessica jerked, exploded, then went stiff.

***

Meanwhile, on the other side of Dallas, Parlay was seated on the Laz-y-Boy inside of his therapist office. He had been checking his phone every five minutes, awaiting an important call or perhaps a text.

"You haven't put that phone down since you walked in," Dr. Haskins said, pouring each of them a cup of coffee.

Parlay shook his head, not wanting to admit if she was wrong or right.

"Just how you like it," she said as she handed him the navy blue coffee mug that had his name imprinted on it. She had gotten it made just for him. Although Parlay wasn't much of a coffee drinker, he had taught her how to make it just how he liked it, whenever he did drink it. Today was one of those days.

"Mel, my gut has never steered me wrong and on top of that, this thing that we have has run its course."

Dr. Haskins and Parlay had formed a bond beyond a client and therapist. She knew the only way she would get him to open up was if she did the same. She had to show him she could be trusted. Mel was short for her middle name, Melanie.

"Divorce is always the last option. That thing, that you refer to it as, is your marriage. How are you so sure? Perhaps the skepticism of infidelity clouds your judgment."

Parlay smacked his lips. "Oh, you really want to know?" He gazed at her as he sat up in his seat. He licked his full lips, then harshly pinched his bottom one. "My dick don't work with her anymore, Mel. Do you know for the longest I thought I had a problem?" He placed a hand over his chest.

Dr. Haskins swallowed the baby lump in her throat. She couldn't envision a man of his quality lacking in an area such as that one. "How are you so for sure it's your wife?" Her brows rose.

"Infidelity, perhaps?" Parlay reclined in his seat. His finger rested against his temple. "I made a vow, a vow I swore to keep. Anything I say, I mean, and if I doubt for one second that I'm not going to be able to stick to it, I ain't gon' agree to it. I don't have to."

Dr. Haskins was impressed, but she would have to continue to veil the truth out of respect for the both of them.

"She thinks it's my meds, Mel, that hinder my sexual abilities. Scientifically its proven to do so. However, an old shorty from my past recently came into my life. Unintentionally, I had been thinking of her the entire time me and my wife had sex."

"Um, okay." She sipped her coffee.

"She had been asking me to stop taking my meds so that I could properly please her, but I couldn't. My struggle is real," he admitted.

Dr. Haskins stood to her feet and started shuffling through some papers on her desk. An idea came to her mind and she needed answers. "So… Is it distaste for your wife, or could it be the utter attraction to ol' girl?" She turned to face him, yet Parlay had answered her question in more ways than one.

"I guess it's just the distaste for my wife, because it seems to work with everyone else." His arms were draped by his side and his bottoms were down at his ankles. His nice-sized dick slightly wagged left to right on its own as he peered at Dr. Haskins lustfully.

Chapter 17
The Perfect Entanglement

Jessica and Jah stood in the semi-dark hallway completely dressed, exchanging saliva. The way they were kissing, you would've thought they were about to have sex rather than just finishing. The doorbell rang. They both paused. Jah's eyes widened and Jessica froze in fear.

"You have to leave." She pushed her towards the bedroom and lifted the window higher.

Jah didn't protest. Jessica rushed to the front. She didn't know who it was, but she had a strong feeling it was Diamond. She didn't even bother to look out the peephole before swinging the door open. Then woman that stood on the other side of the threshold was unfamiliar.

"I'm sorry. Let me introduce myself. I'm Natasha. Parlay asked me to meet him here."

Confusion etched Jessica's face. "Why would he do that?" Jessica asked with attitude. Her mug was so vicious that Natasha began to backpedal. Jealousy pervaded through her like a deadly disease. It was absurd how beautiful she was in spite of the bruises and scars that lingered like an expensive cologne.

"I'm sorry." She turned to leave, but ran right into the arms of Parlay. She gasped and lifted her head to lock eyes with the man she had run from home to be with.

"I'm glad you could make it," he said before leaning down and pecking her cheeks. "Come on," he said taking her by the hand. "I just need to grab a few things." He led her inside, bypassing a baffled Jessica.

"What the fuck are you doing?" She marched behind him.

Parlay spun on his heels swiftly. "I'm done, Jessica. Call that nigga you been fucking," he voiced, then proceeded down the hallways.

"You crazy if you think I'd sleep around on you!" she hollered. Parlay ignored her as he collect items of value. "Parlay!" She ran and stood in front of him. "Parlay!"

"Bruh, move!" He shoved her out of the way. "He must have just left, 'cause you got sex on your breath right now!"

Shamefully, Jessica stopped trying and fell to her knees. She wailed like a newborn child.

"Parlay," she cried repeatedly as she watched him leave their home with another woman. She had committed the ultimate sin, and oddly, Parlay had found out. Unbeknownst to Jessica, there was a multitude of evidence. The lingering masculine fragrance, the sex that cling to her lips, the scent of cigarette smoke, her guilt-filled eyes, and mainly the loud screams that awoke his elderly next door neighbor.

"Parlay, where we going?" Natasha turned and asked him once they were seated in his car.

He gazed into her eyes. The humor behind them was as grand as the smile on his face.

"We going to chill and do us for a week. Once I get word our little problem is taken care of, we're going to shoot back to your city."

Later that night

"Ain't this what you came for
Don't you wish you came more
Girl, what you playing for (oooh)
Come on, come let me kiss that…"

Natasha shivered beneath him as he rocked in and out, side to side, breathtaking strokes. He was gentle, he was patient, he was bigger. He stroked meticulously with purpose. He smelled better, he felt better, he kissed better, he fucked better. A lonesome tear escaped her eyes as she tried her damndest to move to his rhythm rather than lie stiff like a corpse, which seemed easier since each stroke paralyzed her even more. This was only the beginning, yet both of them seemed to be enjoying the present rather than the past. Jessica took a piece of his self-assurance every time she initiated the sex and he failed to meet her needs. Natasha had given him his crown back. She made him whole. Her lips were softer - both sets. Her pussy was wetter. Her ass was fatter, and the sex was so refreshing. It wasn't even about the sex. She knew how to treat him. Her slate was clean in his eyes. Jessica had become extinct the second he found out she had aborted his seed.

Loud smacking noises filled the suite every time their bodies clashed. He thrust forward. She bucked her hips.

They came simultaneously, and both of their bodies went limp.

The End

Acknowledgments

They say motivation only lasts so long, so in the midst of being motivated, it's vital to attain discipline. I want to thank God for physically and mentally strengthening me to do so. Kenny! You a real one. King and Del, I love you all. To those on lock, I 'preciate the support. It's almost over.

Lock Down Publications and Ca$h Presents assisted publishing packages.

BASIC PACKAGE $499
Editing
Cover Design
Formatting

UPGRADED PACKAGE $800
Typing
Editing
Cover Design
Formatting

ADVANCE PACKAGE $1,200
Typing
Editing
Cover Design
Formatting
Copyright registration
Proofreading
Upload book to Amazon

LDP SUPREME PACKAGE $1,500
Typing
Editing
Cover Design
Formatting
Copyright registration
Proofreading
Set up Amazon account

Upload book to Amazon
Advertise on LDP Amazon and Facebook page

***Other services available upon request. Additional charges may apply
Lock Down Publications
P.O. Box 944
Stockbridge, GA 30281-9998
Phone # 470 303-9761

Submission Guideline

Submit the first three chapters of your completed manuscript to ldpsubmissions@gmail.com, subject line: Your book's title. The manuscript must be in a .doc file and sent as an attachment. Document should be in Times New Roman, double spaced and in size 12 font. Also, provide your synopsis and full contact information. If sending multiple submissions, they must each be in a separate email.

Have a story but no way to send it electronically? You can still submit to LDP/Ca$h Presents. Send in the first three chapters, written or typed, of your completed manuscript to:

LDP: Submissions Dept
Po Box 944
Stockbridge, Ga 30281

DO NOT send original manuscript. Must be a duplicate.

Provide your synopsis and a cover letter containing your full contact information.

Thanks for considering LDP and Ca$h Presents.

<u>NEW RELEASES</u>

MONEY MAFIA 2 by JIBRIL WILLIAMS

REAL G'S MOVE IN SILENCE by VON DIESEL

IF YOU CROSS ME ONCE 2 by ANTHONY
FIELDS

PILLOW PRINCESS by S. HAWKINS

Coming Soon from Lock Down Publications/Ca$h Presents

BLOOD OF A BOSS **VI**

SHADOWS OF THE GAME II

TRAP BASTARD II

By **Askari**

LOYAL TO THE GAME **IV**

By **T.J. & Jelissa**

TRUE SAVAGE **VIII**

MIDNIGHT CARTEL IV

DOPE BOY MAGIC IV

CITY OF KINGZ III

NIGHTMARE ON SILENT AVE II

THE PLUG OF LIL MEXICO II

CLASSIC CITY II

By **Chris Green**

BLAST FOR ME **III**

A SAVAGE DOPEBOY III

CUTTHROAT MAFIA III

DUFFLE BAG CARTEL VII

HEARTLESS GOON VI

By **Ghost**

A HUSTLER'S DECEIT III

KILL ZONE II

BAE BELONGS TO ME III

TIL DEATH II

By **Aryanna**

KING OF THE TRAP III

By **T.J. Edwards**
GORILLAZ IN THE BAY V
3X KRAZY III
STRAIGHT BEAST MODE III
De'Kari
KINGPIN KILLAZ IV
STREET KINGS III
PAID IN BLOOD III
CARTEL KILLAZ IV
DOPE GODS III
Hood Rich
SINS OF A HUSTLA II
ASAD
YAYO V
Bred In The Game 2
S. Allen
THE STREETS WILL TALK II
By Yolanda Moore
SON OF A DOPE FIEND III
HEAVEN GOT A GHETTO II
SKI MASK MONEY II
By Renta
LOYALTY AIN'T PROMISED III
By Keith Williams
I'M NOTHING WITHOUT HIS LOVE II
SINS OF A THUG II
TO THE THUG I LOVED BEFORE II

IN A HUSTLER I TRUST II

By Monet Dragun

QUIET MONEY IV

EXTENDED CLIP III

THUG LIFE IV

By **Trai'Quan**

THE STREETS MADE ME IV

By **Larry D. Wright**

IF YOU CROSS ME ONCE III

ANGEL V

By **Anthony Fields**

THE STREETS WILL NEVER CLOSE IV

By K'ajji

HARD AND RUTHLESS III

KILLA KOUNTY IV

By Khufu

MONEY GAME III

By Smoove Dolla

JACK BOYS VS DOPE BOYS IV

A GANGSTA'S QUR'AN V

COKE GIRLZ II

COKE BOYS II

LIFE OF A SAVAGE V

CHI'RAQ GANGSTAS V

By Romell Tukes

MURDA WAS THE CASE III

Elijah R. Freeman

THE STREETS NEVER LET GO III

By Robert Baptiste

AN UNFORESEEN LOVE IV

BABY, I'M WINTERTIME COLD III

By **Meesha**

QUEEN OF THE ZOO III

By **Black Migo**

VICIOUS LOYALTY III

By Kingpen

A GANGSTA'S PAIN III

By J-Blunt

CONFESSIONS OF A JACKBOY III

By Nicholas Lock

GRIMEY WAYS III

By Ray Vinci

KING KILLA II

By Vincent "Vitto" Holloway

BETRAYAL OF A THUG III

By Fre$h

THE MURDER QUEENS III

By Michael Gallon

THE BIRTH OF A GANGSTER III

By Delmont Player

TREAL LOVE II

By Le'Monica Jackson

FOR THE LOVE OF BLOOD III

Pillow Princess

By Jamel Mitchell
RAN OFF ON DA PLUG II
By Paper Boi Rari
HOOD CONSIGLIERE III
By Keese
PRETTY GIRLS DO NASTY THINGS II
By Nicole Goosby
PROTÉGÉ OF A LEGEND II
By Corey Robinson
IT'S JUST ME AND YOU II
By Ah'Million
BORN IN THE GRAVE III
By Self Made Tay
FOREVER GANGSTA III
By Adrian Dulan
GORILLAZ IN THE TRENCHES II
By SayNoMore
THE COCAINE PRINCESS VI
By King Rio
CRIME BOSS II
Playa Ray
LOYALTY IS EVERYTHING II
Molotti
HERE TODAY GONE TOMORROW II
By Fly Rock
REAL G'S MOVE IN SILENCE II
By Von Diesel

<u>Available Now</u>

RESTRAINING ORDER **I & II**
By **CA$H & Coffee**
LOVE KNOWS NO BOUNDARIES **I II & III**
By **Coffee**
RAISED AS A GOON I, II, III & IV
BRED BY THE SLUMS I, II, III
BLAST FOR ME I & II
ROTTEN TO THE CORE I II III
A BRONX TALE I, II, III
DUFFLE BAG CARTEL I II III IV V VI
HEARTLESS GOON I II III IV V
A SAVAGE DOPEBOY I II
DRUG LORDS I II III
CUTTHROAT MAFIA I II
KING OF THE TRENCHES
By **Ghost**
LAY IT DOWN **I & II**
LAST OF A DYING BREED I II
BLOOD STAINS OF A SHOTTA I & II III
By **Jamaica**
LOYAL TO THE GAME I II III

LIFE OF SIN I, II III

By **TJ & Jelissa**

BLOODY COMMAS I & II

SKI MASK CARTEL I II & III

KING OF NEW YORK I II,III IV V

RISE TO POWER I II III

COKE KINGS I II III IV V

BORN HEARTLESS I II III IV

KING OF THE TRAP I II

By **T.J. Edwards**

IF LOVING HIM IS WRONG…I & II

LOVE ME EVEN WHEN IT HURTS I II III

By **Jelissa**

WHEN THE STREETS CLAP BACK I & II III

THE HEART OF A SAVAGE I II III IV

MONEY MAFIA I II

LOYAL TO THE SOIL I II III

By **Jibril Williams**

A DISTINGUISHED THUG STOLE MY HEART I II & III

LOVE SHOULDN'T HURT I II III IV

RENEGADE BOYS I II III IV

PAID IN KARMA I II III

SAVAGE STORMS I II III

AN UNFORESEEN LOVE I II III

BABY, I'M WINTERTIME COLD I II

By **Meesha**

A GANGSTER'S CODE I &, II III

A GANGSTER'S SYN I II III

THE SAVAGE LIFE I II III

CHAINED TO THE STREETS I II III

BLOOD ON THE MONEY I II III

A GANGSTA'S PAIN I II

By J-Blunt

PUSH IT TO THE LIMIT

By **Bre' Hayes**

BLOOD OF A BOSS **I, II, III, IV, V**

SHADOWS OF THE GAME

TRAP BASTARD

By **Askari**

THE STREETS BLEED MURDER **I, II & III**

THE HEART OF A GANGSTA I II& III

By **Jerry Jackson**

CUM FOR ME I II III IV V VI VII VIII

An **LDP Erotica Collaboration**

BRIDE OF A HUSTLA **I II & II**

THE FETTI GIRLS **I, II& III**

CORRUPTED BY A GANGSTA I, II III, IV

BLINDED BY HIS LOVE

THE PRICE YOU PAY FOR LOVE I, II ,III

DOPE GIRL MAGIC I II III

By **Destiny Skai**

WHEN A GOOD GIRL GOES BAD

By **Adrienne**

THE COST OF LOYALTY I II III

By Kweli

A GANGSTER'S REVENGE **I II III & IV**

THE BOSS MAN'S DAUGHTERS I II III IV V

A SAVAGE LOVE **I & II**

BAE BELONGS TO ME I II

A HUSTLER'S DECEIT I, II, III

WHAT BAD BITCHES DO I, II, III

SOUL OF A MONSTER I II III

KILL ZONE

A DOPE BOY'S QUEEN I II III

TIL DEATH

By **Aryanna**

A KINGPIN'S AMBITON

A KINGPIN'S AMBITION **II**

I MURDER FOR THE DOUGH

By **Ambitious**

TRUE SAVAGE I II III IV V VI VII

DOPE BOY MAGIC I, II, III

MIDNIGHT CARTEL I II III

CITY OF KINGZ I II

NIGHTMARE ON SILENT AVE

THE PLUG OF LIL MEXICO II

CLASSIC CITY

By **Chris Green**

A DOPEBOY'S PRAYER

By **Eddie "Wolf" Lee**

THE KING CARTEL **I, II & III**

By **Frank Gresham**

THESE NIGGAS AIN'T LOYAL **I, II & III**

By **Nikki Tee**

GANGSTA SHYT **I II &III**

By **CATO**

THE ULTIMATE BETRAYAL

By **Phoenix**

BOSS'N UP **I , II & III**

By **Royal Nicole**

I LOVE YOU TO DEATH

By **Destiny J**

I RIDE FOR MY HITTA

I STILL RIDE FOR MY HITTA

By **Misty Holt**

LOVE & CHASIN' PAPER

By **Qay Crockett**

TO DIE IN VAIN

SINS OF A HUSTLA

By **ASAD**

BROOKLYN HUSTLAZ

By **Boogsy Morina**

BROOKLYN ON LOCK I & II

By **Sonovia**

GANGSTA CITY

By **Teddy Duke**

A DRUG KING AND HIS DIAMOND I & II III

A DOPEMAN'S RICHES

HER MAN, MINE'S TOO I, II

CASH MONEY HO'S

THE WIFEY I USED TO BE I II

PRETTY GIRLS DO NASTY THINGS

By Nicole Goosby

TRAPHOUSE KING **I II & III**

KINGPIN KILLAZ I II III

STREET KINGS I II

PAID IN BLOOD **I II**

CARTEL KILLAZ I II III

DCPE GODS I II

By **Hood Rich**

LIPSTICK KILLAH **I, II, III**

CRIME OF PASSION I II & III

FRIEND OR FOE I II III

By **Mimi**

STEADY MOBBN' **I, II, III**

THE STREETS STAINED MY SOUL I II III

By **Marcellus Allen**

WHO SHOT YA **I, II, III**

SON OF A DOPE FIEND I II

HEAVEN GOT A GHETTO

SKI MASK MONEY

Renta

GORILLAZ IN THE BAY **I II III IV**

TEARS OF A GANGSTA I II

3X KRAZY I II

STRAIGHT BEAST MODE I II
DE'KARI
TRIGGADALE I II III
MURDAROBER WAS THE CASE I II
Elijah R. Freeman
GOD BLESS THE TRAPPERS I, II, III
THESE SCANDALOUS STREETS I, II, III
FEAR MY GANGSTA I, II, III IV, V
THESE STREETS DON'T LOVE NOBODY I, II
BURY ME A G I, II, III, IV, V
A GANGSTA'S EMPIRE I, II, III, IV
THE DOPEMAN'S BODYGAURD I II
THE REALEST KILLAZ I II III
THE LAST OF THE OGS I II III
Tranay Adams
THE STREETS ARE CALLING
Duquie Wilson
MARRIED TO A BOSS I II III
By Destiny Skai & Chris Green
KINGZ OF THE GAME I II III IV V VI
CRIME BOSS
Playa Ray
SLAUGHTER GANG I II III
RUTHLESS HEART I II III
By Willie Slaughter
FUK SHYT
By Blakk Diamond

DON'T F#CK WITH MY HEART I II

By Linnea

ADDICTED TO THE DRAMA I II III

IN THE ARM OF HIS BOSS II

By Jamila

YAYO I II III IV

A SHOOTER'S AMBITION I II

BRED IN THE GAME

By S. Allen

TRAP GOD I II III

RICH $AVAGE I II III

MONEY IN THE GRAVE I II III

By Martell Troublesome Bolden

FOREVER GANGSTA I II

GLOCKS ON SATIN SHEETS I II

By Adrian Dulan

TOE TAGZ I II III IV

LEVELS TO THIS SHYT I II

IT'S JUST ME AND YOU

By Ah'Million

KINGPIN DREAMS I II III

RAN OFF ON DA PLUG

By Paper Boi Rari

CONFESSIONS OF A GANGSTA I II III IV

CONFESSIONS OF A JACKBOY I II

By Nicholas Lock

I'M NOTHING WITHOUT HIS LOVE

SINS OF A THUG
TO THE THUG I LOVED BEFORE
A GANGSTA SAVED XMAS
IN A HUSTLER I TRUST
By Monet Dragun
CAUGHT UP IN THE LIFE I II III
THE STREETS NEVER LET GO I II
By Robert Baptiste
NEW TO THE GAME I II III
MONEY, MURDER & MEMORIES I II III
By **Malik D. Rice**
LIFE OF A SAVAGE I II III IV
A GANGSTA'S QUR'AN I II III IV
MURDA SEASON I II III
GANGLAND CARTEL I II III
CHI'RAQ GANGSTAS I II III IV
KILLERS ON ELM STREET I II III
JACK BOYZ N DA BRONX I II III
A DOPEBOY'S DREAM I II III
JACK BOYS VS DOPE BOYS I II III
COKE GIRLZ
COKE BOYS
By Romell Tukes
LOYALTY AIN'T PROMISED I II
By Keith Williams
QUIET MONEY I II III
THUG LIFE I II III

EXTENDED CLIP I II

A GANGSTA'S PARADISE

By **Trai'Quan**

THE STREETS MADE ME I II III

By **Larry D. Wright**

THE ULTIMATE SACRIFICE I, II, III, IV, V, VI

KHADIFI

IF YOU CROSS ME ONCE I II

ANGEL I II III IV

IN THE BLINK OF AN EYE

By **Anthony Fields**

THE LIFE OF A HOOD STAR

By Ca$h & Rashia Wilson

THE STREETS WILL NEVER CLOSE I II III

By K'ajji

CREAM I II III

THE STREETS WILL TALK

By Yolanda Moore

NIGHTMARES OF A HUSTLA I II III

By King Dream

CONCRETE KILLA I II III

VICIOUS LOYALTY I II

By Kingpen

HARD AND RUTHLESS I II

MOB TOWN 251

THE BILLIONAIRE BENTLEYS I II III

REAL G'S MOVE IN SILENCE

By Von Diesel

GHOST MOB

Stilloan Robinson

MOB TIES I II III IV V VI

SOUL OF A HUSTLER, HEART OF A KILLER

GORILLAZ IN THE TRENCHES

By SayNoMore

BODYMORE MURDERLAND I II III

THE BIRTH OF A GANGSTER I II

By Delmont Player

FOR THE LOVE OF A BOSS

By C. D. Blue

MOBBED UP I II III IV

THE BRICK MAN I II III IV V

THE COCAINE PRINCESS I II III IV V

By King Rio

KILLA KOUNTY I II III IV

By Khufu

MONEY GAME I II

By Smoove Dolla

A GANGSTA'S KARMA I II III

By FLAME

KING OF THE TRENCHES I II III

by **GHOST & TRANAY ADAMS**

QUEEN OF THE ZOO I II

By **Black Migo**

GRIMEY WAYS I II

By Ray Vinci

XMAS WITH AN ATL SHOOTER

By Ca$h & Destiny Skai

KING KILLA

By Vincent "Vitto" Holloway

BETRAYAL OF A THUG I II

By Fre$h

THE MURDER QUEENS I II

By Michael Gallon

TREAL LOVE

By Le'Monica Jackson

FOR THE LOVE OF BLOOD I II

By Jamel Mitchell

HOOD CONSIGLIERE I II

By Keese

PROTÉGÉ OF A LEGEND

By Corey Robinson

BORN IN THE GRAVE I II

By Self Made Tay

MOAN IN MY MOUTH

By XTASY

TORN BETWEEN A GANGSTER AND A GENTLEMAN

By J-BLUNT & Miss Kim

LOYALTY IS EVERYTHING

Molotti

HERE TODAY GONE TOMORROW

By Fly Rock

PILLOW PRINCESS
By S. Hawkins

<u>BOOKS BY LDP'S CEO, CA$H</u>

TRUST IN NO MAN

TRUST IN NO MAN 2

TRUST IN NO MAN 3

BONDED BY BLOOD

SHORTY GOT A THUG

THUGS CRY

THUGS CRY 2

THUGS CRY 3

TRUST NO BITCH

TRUST NO BITCH 2

TRUST NO BITCH 3

TIL MY CASKET DROPS

RESTRAINING ORDER

RESTRAINING ORDER 2

IN LOVE WITH A CONVICT

LIFE OF A HOOD STAR

XMAS WITH AN ATL SHOOTER

S. Hawkins